BETWEEN EMPIRES AND CONTINENTS

A Luxor City Novel

Sasha Hope

A NineStar Press Publication

www.ninestarpress.com

Between Empires and Continents

Printed in the USA

ISBN: 978-1-64890-281-9

First Edition, May, 2021

Also available in eBook, ISBN: 978-1-64890-280-2

WARNING:

This book contains sexually explicit material, which is only suitable for mature readers, scenes of violence and death, guns, and human trafficking.

*To everyone who read The Empires of Luxor City.
Here's to coming back for more!*

One:The Underground

The Southern Empire glittered like a neon jewel at the tip of the vast island metropolis that was Luxor City, offering visitors and locals alike a chance to live another life. Between the intersections of technicolor streets, every threshold was another opportunity to experience the height of southern entertainment and luxury. The South's booming city center was a shining district renowned for its fine dining and nightlife. People from all over the world sailed for weeks just to pay a visit. But, as is the trouble in all cities, dark corners filled space among the shadows cast by dazzling lights.

Junsu Sun was proud of the Empire he would one day inherit. Recent increases in corruption were no surprise in a city founded largely on the drug trade between Luxor and the Second Continent. Still, Junsu wasn't pleased to find out just how deep the opium-coated rabbit hole went. The underground world that had been built up in the back alleys between skyscrapers both enraged and fascinated him to no end.

Since the unification of Luxor City and the newfound peace between the island's three territories—North, Central, and South—Junsu had been on a quest to know more about his Empire and the inner workings of their expansive business. As the sole heir to Xijuan Sun, the aging Alpha of the Southern Empire, he was starting to feel the weight of duty falling more and more heavily upon his shoulders. Despite only occupying the southern tip of Luxor City, the territory his family's Empire encompassed was vast and densely populated.

Junsu had no idea what went down in some of the red-light hotspots dotting the city's entertainment district, but over the past few weeks he'd been carefully slipping into the inner circles of some of the city's most notorious gangsters, learning more and more about the Southern underbelly, what the Sun family and their allies simply called the Underground.

This was how he found himself sitting around a table playing Mah-jongg with a group of Alphas his mother would have killed as soon as she'd looked at them. These were members of the Underground, people whose fidelity to the Sun family was always in question. They stepped around rules and edicts to run their shady district nightclubs off the grid.

This evening, however, they were all sitting together glowering at Mah-jongg tiles with knowing black eyes.

Four Alphas were seated as is required in Mah-jongg, one person per side of a perfectly square table: North, South, East and West. Junsu occupied the East seat. He leaned into a soft chair with its back to a large loading bay door. Though prominent industrial pieces of architecture were blatantly scattered about the Underground hideout, there was a luxury apparent in the chic den only the highest rollers could afford. Eccentric art pieces decorated the walls and were often lit with neon beams, adding ambience to the eclectic atmosphere.

Junsu hadn't been expecting this Underground gang to literally be inside an underground venue, but he found something vaguely amusing about their headquarters. In the darkness, dull violet lights illuminated the faces of gamblers and socialites. Their smirking features glowed in an ominous manner. The exposed piping above their table rattled and hissed, probably taking on the tide water from the nearby shoreline. The noise was almost drowned out by the pounding music coming from the club on the floor above.

Junsu stared down at his onyx and jade Mah-jongg tiles, running his thumb over one of the gold-painted engravings marking it. He smiled at his latest pick and flipped his pieces down onto the table, showing off the winning hand.

"My game again," he uttered before reaching a lazy hand over to his drink. He hid a smirk around the rim of his glass as the rest of the Alphas at the table groaned.

Junsu, the newcomer, had won his third game in a row.

"You know, Sun. It's only polite to let your elders win sometimes," the middle-aged man at the West side of the table grunted around the end of a newly lit cigarette. He was the Underground's leader, an Alpha called Naoto Kim. His wrinkled features were drawn up in a smirk, visibly amused by Junsu's luck even while his eyes were narrowed with a hint of suspicion.

Junsu could see it, but he simply chuckled and moved his tiles back into the center of the table. He was lucky to have secured this meeting with Naoto Kim, but he wasn't about to lose on purpose just to stroke the other Alpha's ego.

"My mother is a good teacher," Junsu murmured as he drew a hand over the tiles, mixing them about over the velvet-covered tabletop. In contrast to this venue, his mother had a few high-tech tables back in the casino capable of shuffling themselves. Her tables moved the tiles into a mechanical repository under the green velvet before restacking and dealing them out in neat piles. Naoto's club was a little *passé,* but Junsu was polite enough not to mention it.

Naoto's lazy gaze traced Junsu's hand as it moved over the tiles while he shuffled. With gritted teeth, he laughed to himself before taking a long drag off his cigarette. Smoke billowed from between his lips, momentarily obscuring his glaring eyes.

"I bet you regret inviting the Sun kid over for playtime now. Hey, Seijin?" Tae, the man on the North side of the table, said to the man at the South.

Seijin didn't look too happy. As a younger member of the gang, his pockets weren't anywhere near as loaded as his fellows' and Junsu had practically emptied them out.

Junsu had met Seijin through a contact who'd infiltrated the Underground. Buddying up to the young Alpha had been a cinch. After a few meetups, money had exchanged hands and Junsu eventually convinced Seijin to let him in on one of their Mah-jongg games to give him a chance to meet with Naoto Kim. Junsu had a particular interest in the Underground membership and their trade. They were an up-and-coming group and, despite the conflict between the Underground and the Sun family, Junsu had paid great attention to their business.

"Look, Junsu didn't come here to play Mah-jongg. All right, Tae?" Seijin snapped back. "He's not just here to fleece me."

"Seijin's right," Junsu said with a nod. He tossed a few tiles across the table with an absent flick of the wrist. "I didn't come here to play. I came for business."

Naoto stared at him, still glaring down the end of his cigarette. "Not sure if we need your mother's business," he muttered in response.

"Not hers. Mine," Junsu replied curtly.

The other men looked to their leader as Naoto hummed softly. "I know for a fact that Xijuan Sun would not be happy to hear her only son is trying to make deals on the side with people she doesn't have much of a fondness for," he murmured. "Your Omega mother was killed by outsiders like us back in the day. Since then, your family hasn't let a single group form within the bounds of the Southern Empire without their knowledge."

"Not to mention a hefty amount of oversight," Seijin grunted.

Naoto pointed his cigarette in Seijin's direction as he spoke. "Exactly. Oversight is bad for business. We get by just fine without you and your family, so unless you're here to start shit, drop it. Let's all play another round, and you can give us a chance to win our money back."

Junsu took another sip of his drink, attempting to hide the shiver that ran through his core at the mention of his deceased parent. His Omega mother, Lian Sun, had died back when he was too young to even remember her. He'd heard his Alpha mother, Xijuan, tell the story a thousand times. A turf war had been taken too far and an assassination on Xijuan had missed its mark one afternoon. At the opening of a newly refurbished shipping yard, Xijuan had brought her Omega along and was showing her off in front of a crowd when the shot was fired.

The bullet meant for Xijuan had missed her...but it hit Lian.

Junsu had been at home with the nanny when it happened and while he didn't remember his Omega mother, he remembered the panic of that day. The crying. The shouting. The bloodstains on Xijuan's white silk coat. The horror of it still flooded his mind.

The Southern Empire used to allow for competition among the dealers and tradespeople, but after the death of Lian Sun that all ended. After her death, well, the crime lords on the streets were either members of the Sun Family or they worked for the Sun Family, but they never, ever tried to start up their own mob or work against the Sun Family.

Xijuan Sun took on a scorched-earth policy when it came to the black markets. That policy had moved people like Naoto and his cronies deep underground.

"I know for a fact you do your dirty deals on my family's turf," Junsu replied after a moment of silence. He let his words echo Naoto's, drawing a huff from the man.

He ignored Seijin as the Alpha cast him a nervous glance. A few of the other Underground members around them sat back in their seats, fingers visibly itching to reach for weapons hidden beneath the fabric of their bespoke suits.

Junsu went on despite the growing tension. "You forget that people outside the Sun family aren't the only ones who want more than what they've managed to scrape up. I'm done being my mother's lackey, waiting for my turn to take over. I'm done doing what's best for Luxor rather than what's best for the South since this whole—" he waved a passive hand and spat out the word "—unification."

Naoto raised a dark brow. He, like everyone else in Luxor City, was well aware of the fact that Junsu Sun had played a pivotal role in orchestrating said unification. The Alpha leaders of Luxor City's three Empires—Faraji in the

North, Wesa in the Center, and Sun in the South—had, after many long, tense years, recently signed new trade deals to help grease the once-rusted wheels of commerce throughout the city. But those deals had come with restrictions on the Southern Empire's drug industry, forcing it to go legal and regulate. The process pissed off quite a few of the Southern kingpins.

Now the same Junsu Sun who had helped unify the city and get these unideal trade agreements was staring at a group of minor-league crime lords saying, "I want in."

Again, all eyes shifted to Naoto.

The older man's expression didn't change, his deadpan gaze gave away nothing, but Junsu knew better. He knew Naoto Kim and his Underground gang needed someone to give them validation if they wanted to get anywhere in the Southern Empire. They needed both respect and leverage over Xijuan Sun. It was one thing to take on the Sun Family and invite an entire army to rise up against them, it was entirely another to take on the Sun Family with the heir to said family, tearing it apart from the inside before picking up the pieces for themselves.

They needed Junsu Sun and he knew it.

"Tell me about your trade," Junsu asked. "What do you deal in? Who do you work with on the Southern ships and ports?"

Seijin whispered something to Naoto in a language Junsu was not as familiar with. Naoto gave a barely visible nod before leaning back to let his underling explain.

"We shouldn't get into ports and such just yet, but our trade is in...well, upstairs is a brothel, so you can't be too surprised."

Junsu breathed deeply, calming his frayed nerves. "You trade in people."

"Omegas," Naoto replied, as if they were not one and the same. "Let's not beat around the proverbial bush, Sun. We import from the Second Continent. Omegas are easy to come by and they don't have the same rights over there. Still, they're good, fine quality Omegas."

"All willing, of course," Seijin cut in awkwardly. "They want to come here. Better life in New America and all that shit."

Naoto waved that off, as if it could be left unsaid.

Junsu felt his mask of indifference slipping. He tried not to let his brow crease into a frown. He couldn't let on that he wasn't exactly keen on Naoto's line of work. "So, you hire Omegas, sneak them into the city without papers."

"Some of them have papers, but if they don't, we know a guy who can provide," Tae spoke up then. He shrugged his shoulders as if he wasn't just admitting to disobeying an age-old law that had been in place in all of Luxor City well before last year's unification. No one got in without the right travel papers.

Still, Junsu only nodded along to the oncoming tune of this disturbing information.

"So, you bring them over and put them to work upstairs," he murmured, clarifying it for himself more than anything. "Can they leave?"

"I don't see why they'd want to," Naoto drawled. "The job pays well. But they can leave as long as they pay us back what they owe for the lodging, transportation, paperwork..."

"How long does that usually take?" Junsu cut in.

Naoto waved off the question and went on. "The job pays well. We earn our share taking a cut off the top for the protection, management, utilities..."

"And what they're left with is what? Barely enough to pay for a meal?" Junsu snapped. His words made those around him tense. They were expecting him to come to understand the terms of their trade, not criticize it.

While his men shifted uncomfortably in their seats, Naoto simply shrugged, becoming more and more brazen. "Every once in a while, we sell an Omega off to the highest bidder. We usually transfer their debt to the buyer, whoever that is. It's a pretty nice step up in the world for a poor Omega from those busy city streets in the Second Continent. We're practically a charity." He chuckled around the end of his cigarette. "You're not mated, are you, Junsu?"

"No," Junsu said. His voice grew dark, monotone.

"I didn't think so," Naoto said while nodding. "Too busy running the South. Well, I can sweeten part of this deal for you. Give you your pick of any of the Omegas in the house on the house." He laughed at his little play on words and his men laughed along with him like the sycophants they were. "Like I said, we've got some of the finest Second Continent Omegas you've ever seen. You can even try a few out before you settle on one that you like."

Try before you buy. Junsu wanted to be sick.

He leaned back in his seat, eerily quiet. He sensed Seijin starting to get more and more agitated; the man was twitching in the chair beside him as if his seat was made of pins and needles.

"What do you say, Junsu?" he asked suddenly, unable to handle the silence. "It's a pretty good deal, plus a cut of the profits—"

"I don't want your fucking profits."

The venom with which Junsu spat out these words had both Seijin and Tae on their feet. Their sudden movement drew the notice of other members of the gang scattered throughout the small room. The ambient din of chatter died and the silence that lingered hung heavy in the air.

Naoto continued to stare at Junsu through a thick cloud of tobacco smoke. He hadn't said anything, but his knowing gaze weighed heavy. After taking another long, pointed drag on his cigarette, he blew the smoke into Junsu's unfazed face.

"Why'd you come here, then?" Naoto spat. "If it was just to make a point, I hope it was worth it."

A few of the gang members chuckled. They could probably see their leader's hand reaching for something under the table. Junsu noticed it too. He spotted the man's movement, and he knew what was coming. This wouldn't be the first time he had a gun to his head.

Still, he sat stoic and straight in his seat. Without breaking eye contact with Naoto, he sipped the last of his drink, set the glass down, and smiled.

"I just wanted to see where the party was at," Junsu said.

Before Naoto or anyone else could even react, the loading bay door behind their table burst open. The heavy clatter of the metal shutter rattled the room before it was drowned out by a rain of bullets and gunfire.

Junsu sat in the midst of the chaos, his composure unruffled. He poured himself another drink from the decanter next to the Mah-jongg table and by the time he'd downed the glass there was no more Naoto Kim and no more Underground.

The air stilled at the moment of ceasefire. Junsu found himself surrounded by a geared-up team of soldiers. The red LEDs of their laser sights were visible here and there through the clouds of smoke and debris. The soldiers scanned the room around him, looking for any remaining Underground agents.

Lowering her gun, one of the soldiers turned toward his seat. "We got 'em all, boss," she said.

"Good work, Hong," Junsu uttered on an exhale as he set down his glass.

"Next orders?"

As the soldier, Hong, approached him, Junsu stood.

"Some of you stay and clean this place up. The rest go clear out the rooms upstairs. Make sure the Omegas are taken to care facilities. If the ones in the South are full, the Center has already agreed to take the rest."

"What do we do with the johns, boss?" she replied with disgust lacing her tone.

Junsu clasped his hands behind his back. "We can let them live, but I want them to know they've done business with people on the wrong side of the Sun family. Any ideas on how we can let them know we don't care for that sort of thing, Hong?"

He couldn't actually see Hong's features through her headgear, but somehow, he knew she was grinning.

"I can think of plenty, boss."

"Ingenuity." Junsu patted her on the shoulder. "That's why I like you, Hong." With a chuckle, he turned to leave through the blasted bay doors.

At the top of the slope that led down into the underground, one of his armed soldiers tossed Junsu a set of keys. He caught them before hopping into a waiting lowrider. The engine started automatically, and the chromium door closed with the click of a button. Junsu sighed, put his hands on the wheel, and began the drive home.

Two: A Business Arrangement

On the western edge of the city where the Southern Empire touched the emerald green of the West Island, Junsu Sun lived in a shining glass home that was the *ne plus ultra* of modern architecture. There were sayings about people who live in glass houses, but as a Sun and the heir to the Southern Empire, Junsu could afford the luxury and everything that came with it.

The morning light rose behind the house in the early hours and the Pacific shone a clear crisp blue. Its foamy white waves rolled up against the seaweed-green rocks along the shore. To one side, the cliffs and greenery of the West Island spanned the distance. The rest of the panorama was filled by a rocky beach and the shimmering vastness of the ocean.

Junsu stood barefoot in the open doorway surrounded by floor-to-ceiling walls of glass. He gazed out over the calming waves, sipping a cup of brown rice tea as a piece of driftwood washed closer and closer up onto the beach with each shove of salty seawater.

He didn't often get to enjoy the calm of his home; even that very morning he would have to leave in about an hour to drive downtown. His mother was expecting him in her office, patiently awaiting his update on the bust from the night before.

Junsu tossed back the last of his tea, set the fine porcelain cup down, and went to get dressed. He shrugged off his robe and showered quickly, shaving in the bath, before slipping into a sharply tailored suit. Like every Alpha leader in Luxor City, Junsu dressed with class. His bespoke suit cut a clean and powerful silhouette, framing his strong figure.

Once dressed, Junsu gave himself a quick once-over in the mirror. He rubbed two fingers along the angle of his freshly shaved jawline, checking for stubble before he sorted out his hair by running his fingers back through the midnight-black strands. With a few comb throughs, he managed to get his quiff to stay in some semblance of a style.

"Good enough," he muttered to himself.

As he went to pluck up his keys, a lean white cat bounded over and curled herself against his legs. She definitely knew he was heading out and seemed to be trying to persuade him not to, as she did every morning.

"Ah! Noon, you're going to mess up my suit," Junsu laughed. His mother had gotten him the cat as a housewarming present. The little snowball wasn't exactly great to have around black suits, but she was a shorthair so Junsu could live with it.

He gave Noon a few placating pets before heading out. He'd not been a big fan of the cat at first, but now, every day, Noon's soft meows behind him broke his heart a little as he closed the door.

*

Junsu took the winding coastal road to the highway and arrived downtown a little before ten. His mother's office was on the top floor of the tallest building in the South, a twisting skyrise that looked like someone had tried to wring out a narrow glass pyramid. It sat dead center in the middle of their Empire. Xijuan always liked to call it her perfect vantage point, but everything below melded into a blur of color from that high up.

Junsu took the glass elevator to his mother's office. He leaned with his back to the door, staring out over the prism of fractal reflections lighting the city skyline in a brilliant holographic glow. The morning's pink-blue hues painted the entire Empire with a wash of violet.

The elevator doors opened right into his mother's office and she was there to greet him with a single clap of her hands. Elegant as always, Xijuan was dressed in a red silk pantsuit and seemed to be just out of another meeting.

"Junsu, well done," she said in a proud but tranquil tone.

Junsu smiled a subtle grin and nodded. "Naoto Kim and his particularly vile faction of the Underground won't be bothering us anymore," he told her. "Any victims are in the appropriate care facilities and we'll get real papers written up for any of the Omegas who don't want to be brought back home to the Second Continent."

"Good," Xijuan replied curtly. "We don't need Naoto and his sort on our streets, not in this new dawn of unification." She chuckled the last word and waved her hand in a dramatic gesture. "We're all meant to be doing our bit for the greater good of Luxor. Never thought I'd live to see the day." Again, Xijuan tittered to herself. "Anyway, we can use this as leverage at the next meeting with the North and Center. I'd love to see Dominik Wesa try to implement that damned narcotics tax of his after we bring them this. Did you find out who Naoto's partners were at the ports or any of his other contacts in the city?"

"No," Junsu replied. His brow furrowed. "I may have called the team in too soon."

After that last game of Mah-jongg, Junsu had dropped his guise too quickly. He probably could have gotten a lot more out of Naoto before calling the team in, but hearing the way the man talked about Omegas, what he and his Alphas were doing with them, had made Junsu act on impulse.

"Ah, my boy. You're so hasty. Just like your mother," Xijuan laughed before letting out a sigh. "Come sit down. I have something important I need to discuss with you. It's a new task and I expect it to take priority. Effective immediately."

Xijuan was grinning as if she'd just told a particularly funny joke, but Junsu didn't get it and was too tired to figure out why. The thought of a new mission was exhausting, especially after the weeks upon weeks of effort he'd put into this last one. After days of undercover operations and back-alley dealings, he had been looking forward to finishing up this meeting as soon as possible so he and his team could celebrate the Underground takedown.

"Mother..." he groaned.

"Junsu..." Xijuan whined in reply. They might have been the leaders of a great Empire, but they were still family, and family knew just how to poke each other's buttons. "You are the heir to the Southern Empire and sometimes that means business will require you when you don't feel like it. Now come," she snapped at him, leaving no room to argue a second time around.

With yet another, more subtle sigh, Junsu followed his mother to her desk. He winced as she gently patted his cheek on her way past him. She sat behind her polished blackwood desk, the shining surface reflecting her dour features in the space between them.

"All right, fine. What's this new mission you have for me?" Junsu muttered as he took a seat in one of Xijuan's elaborate chairs. "Tear down another Underground gang? Check out a new shipment? Throw myself into the sea?"

Xijuan raised a spike-nailed finger, silencing him. She leaned over to open one of the desk drawers and, after having a bit of a rifle around, she produced a thick black folder. It was made with some kind of heavy-looking card, like a vintage photo album of some sort.

"What's this?" Junsu said as he took the folder his mother had slid across the desk toward him.

"Now, Junsu," Xijuan started slowly. "What do you think of this young man?"

With a raised brow Junsu opened the folder. The photograph inside was extremely formal, which was a given since it had been printed and delivered to his mother in a way that just wasn't typically done anymore. Printed pictures were, well, pretty vintage. Whoever sent it clearly hadn't heard of email.

The young man in the portrait was fair with short dark hair and hooded black eyes. His manner of dress was something Junsu hadn't seen in the Southern Empire outside of maybe a museum or a history documentary. The silky violet fabric of his robe was folded across his chest in several layers and tied at the waist with a thick band that corseted his already trim little form.

He was absolutely stunning. Beautiful. Probably an Omega. He was certainly too small to be an Alpha and Junsu had never seen a Beta so pretty. He had a strong desire to see the young man's neck, check if he was already bonded, but in the picture his figure was covered fully beneath the lavender-colored robe from wrists to chin by a thick white turtleneck undershirt.

"So," Xijuan cut in, interrupting his train of thought. "Your thoughts?"

Junsu looked up at her briefly before turning his gaze back to the photograph in his hands. He pursed his lips and shrugged.

"He doesn't seem like he could pose much of a threat, but if you need him dealt with it shouldn't be too—" As he spoke, Junsu looked back up. The look on his mother's face caused him to pause midsentence. Her eyes were wide, and her brows were in her hairline. The aghast expression of horror etched into her features came as a surprise.

Junsu looked into her startled eyes and asked, "What?"

"God, no! Junsu! No, no, no!" Xijuan spluttered, shaking her head at him as if she couldn't believe the words that had just come out of his mouth. There was silence for a moment while she sucked in a deep breath to calm down.

Junsu mirrored her, shaking his head, utterly confused. "Am I missing something?"

Sighing heavily, Xijuan tried again. "What do you *think* of him?" This time when she spoke, she put a pointed emphasis on the word and stared into her son's eyes as if begging him to read between the lines.

Junsu looked down at the picture again. "Oh," he breathed.

Realization forced itself on him like a bullet to the head. His eyes widened as he stared down at the young man, this time taking him in with a completely different point of view. He had thought it was a bit weird. Usually, his mother would just text him a file if there were any targets she needed dealt with. So, this clearly wasn't a photo of a target. Which meant it had to be...

"Oh," Junsu said again, softer this time. "Shit."

The mental switch from "easy kill" to "potential mate" was a full one-eighty, but he got there in the end. Sucking in a breath, he looked to his mother and asked, "He's an Omega?"

"Yes, son."

"You want me to bond with him?"

"Precisely." Xijuan smiled.

"It's not for business, is it?"

"Well, if that makes it easier."

Junsu set the picture aside for a moment, placing it onto the table as far out of his reach as he could muster. He'd come around, sure, but he wasn't exactly thrilled by the turn of events. With wide eyes, he stared straight ahead and ran a hand through his hair. He sat back in his chair and exhaled heavily, trying to get everything straight in his mind. The shift in his composure clearly didn't go unnoticed.

"Look, Junsu," Xijuan said, cutting into the obvious anxiety attack unravelling that Junsu wasn't even trying to hide. "You know I would typically never rush you to bond with anyone under any circumstances, at least not until you were closer to taking over. However, this is political. We need this."

"Need or want?" Junsu snapped back. When his mother's dark eyes twitched slightly, he quieted down and gestured for her to proceed.

"I *need* you to understand. This is a match made in heaven. This boy is the finest Omega in the Second Continent. You're never going to do any better."

Junsu huffed at that. Admittedly, if the photograph did him justice, this young man was one of the most beautiful Omegas he'd ever seen and he'd seen Lin Wesa. Dominik Wesa was a lucky man up there in the Central Empire, but Junsu wouldn't feel remotely inferior standing next to him at the city galas with this young man on his arm.

"Who is he?"

"His name is Kaito. Kaito Yamaguchi."

"Yamaguchi?" Junsu repeated. "As in *Yamaguchi* Yamaguchi?"

"Yes. From the Yamaguchi family of the Second Continent's big islands. His parents are Shen and Kazue Yamaguchi. They are the current heads of the family and the proprietors of the business throughout the Second Continent."

Junsu nodded. He knew the Yamaguchi family; everyone knew the Yamaguchi family. They were just like the Sun, or the Wesa or the Faraji, but exponentially larger. The Yamaguchi ruled an Empire like they all did in Luxor, but while the Sun family micromanaged their little sections of a vast island city, the Yamaguchi ran an entire continent.

From their home in the Eastern Capital to the edge of the Golden Desert, the Yamaguchi family was large and well connected. However, their Empire was chaotic, and coming from someone from a city like Luxor, that was saying something. Where every Empire in Luxor made a point to have a single Alpha heir to provide quick and easy successions, the Yamaguchi family and their extended relatives often fought for power amongst themselves.

A few years back, when the previous Yamaguchi Alpha passed away, rumors of chaos spreading throughout the Second Continent had reached all the way to Luxor. Junsu remembered it vividly because their import pipeline from the Second Continent had broken down for an entire month. Most journalists were too scared and rightly cautious to report in depth on what exactly had happened to quell the mayhem in the family. Needless to say, the current Alpha, Kazue Yamaguchi, used to have at least three more brothers than she did now.

"Kaito is the third son of Shen and Kazue Yamaguchi and he—"

"Wait. The third son?" Junsu raised a brow, trying his best to feign disgrace. "If we're going to be old-fashioned, shouldn't this trade-off be one for one? A first for a first? At least a second…"

"If you want to mate with an Alpha, then by all means, Junsu, I'll arrange it," his mother retorted, rolling her eyes.

Junsu pursed his lips. His mother knew he wasn't interested in other Alphas. An Alpha and an Alpha together wasn't entirely taboo, but it wasn't exactly common. He was fond of Omegas, any gender, Junsu wasn't picky. He knew he'd settle down with an Omega one day, but he'd also dabbled with a Beta or two in the past.

Xijuan clearly noted his expression and took it as a sign to go on. "Kaito is the first Omega born into the direct Yamaguchi family line for centuries," she said. "This arrangement is a great honor for us." She fixed Junsu with a deathly serious gaze. "The news of Luxor City's most eligible Alphas getting snatched up one by one these last few years has gone international. First Dominik Wesa and his little flower from the Mainland and now just last year

Jimena Faraji and the Wesa family Omega. You are the last and the Yamaguchi family are interested." A smirk twisted Xijuan's lips. "They are our largest and wealthiest trading partners, Junsu. You have to understand how incredibly important this is."

"I do, I do, it's just that—" Junsu stopped with a low groan and brought a hand up to rub at his temples. He didn't really have any excuses apart from the fact that he didn't want to be mated just yet. "This whole thing is so archaic."

He picked up the picture again. The young man in the black circular frame stared back at him with a soft, appealing gaze, but he wasn't smiling about any of this either.

"It's not as if I'm marrying you off to some picture bride looking for a better life in New America," Xijuan huffed. "Kaito Yamaguchi comes from class. Their family compound alone makes our houses look like fucking cottages. Consider this as part of a trade deal. Good for business."

"Good for business?" Junsu raised a brow. "Does this Yamaguchi Omega come with a dowry too? I didn't know we needed the cash."

His mother mocked his expression with a raised brow of her own. "We always need more cash, Junsu. That's how business works."

Junsu groaned. He gave the picture one last look before moving to hand it back to his mother.

"All right, I'll do it."

Xijuan smiled but made no move to take the frame. With a wave of her hand, she said, "Keep it."

"Why?"

"You'll need to know what he looks like. I want you to go meet him."

"What? When?"

Xijuan clicked her tongue and pulled out her phone. After a few taps on the screen, her expression flipped yet again to a grin.

"You leave Monday morning."

"Monday? Are you serious?" Junsu baulked at the information. No wonder she'd wanted to talk to him about it so soon. "It's Friday! That's barely even a weekend away!" He thought he'd at least get some warning before completely giving up his freedom to the lifetime commitment of a bond with an Omega he hadn't even met yet.

Much to his dismay, his mother waved off his concerns. "I'm putting you on one of the luxury cruise liners with a small security detail of your choosing. You'll have an entire week to relax as you make your way to the Eastern Capital. There, you'll have a day to do whatever you like on shore and then you'll meet Kaito at the dock and sail back together."

Great, an entire week to angst. Junsu held back a groan. He didn't want to mope about this; it wasn't as if he was a romantic or anything. He'd fucked around, sure, but there hadn't been a single person he'd developed a long-term relationship with, and it wasn't as if he had any grand dreams of one day meeting the love of his life. Still, inviting a new person into his world like this wasn't exactly how he pictured his future.

With a relenting shrug, he nodded to his mother. "I guess I'll go start packing then. Gotta find someone to watch the house. Take care of the cat," he muttered, slumping back in his chair.

"Oh, don't make that face, Junsu." Xijuan mimicked his pout. "Think of the business. It'll be booming once you have Kazue Yamaguchi as a mother-in-law."

Junsu took a deep breath and nodded again. He solemnly fixed his posture.

Everything was for the family business. Luxor City, the Southern Empire, the business, those aspects of Junsu's life were the be all and end all.

"Do you know if he—is he at least—you know." Junsu winced and made a vague gesture he was sure would be almost completely impossible to decipher.

"Willing?" his mother suggested with an arched brow.

Junsu pointed at that, though he was unable to keep from cringing.

"I assure you, Kaito is in the exact same position you're in." Xijuan actually smiled. "Isn't that nice? Maybe the two of you can bond over it."

"Great," Junsu muttered. "Well, I guess that's it. I'm getting mated."

Xijuan clapped her hands. "I'm so incredibly happy for you both. I'm sure you'll be positively adorable together."

Junsu grunted in response but didn't dare disagree with his mother.

Placing his hands on his thighs, he leaned forward, moving to stand.

"Is that all for today?"

Giving her answer in motion, his mother stood, implying he could as well. She walked around the desk and ushered him toward her. He took a single step forward, standing at eye level with his mother. She put her hands on his shoulders and smiled so fondly he didn't know what to think. She'd never looked at him like that before.

"I'm very proud, you know," she told him. "You've always been such a playboy, I never thought I'd live to see you settle down."

Junsu forced a smile. "Well, I learn from the best," he shot back.

Xijuan made a dismissive sound in the back of her throat. Waving her hands in the air, she walked Junsu back to the elevator shaft, talking all the way.

"I want you packed and ready to leave bright and early Monday morning. I'll have a driver sent to make sure you don't miss it. It's a cruise so bring your best clothes and don't forget a swimming costume."

"Yes, mother." Junsu bowed his head slightly to hide a smirk when she briefly looked back at him. He was thirty now and it always amused him when his mother talked to him as if he were still a child. Then again, he was still her child and always would be in her eyes.

"And this weekend I want you to go out and buy something nice, or better yet, have something made for Kaito."

"Mom," Junsu groaned. "Can't you just have someone do that? You probably know more about him than I do and I just—I just want to enjoy the weekend." It was his last weekend of freedom after all.

"No, it should be you, Junsu," Xijuan snapped in reply. "And make it something classy, elegant, something from the South. His favorite color is purple, or so his father tells me."

Thinking back to the deep-violet silk Kaito wore in the photograph, Junsu couldn't say he was surprised by the information. He did look nice in purple.

"All right," he relented.

"That's my boy." When they reached the elevator, Xijuan turned to him and patted his cheek softly. "Now go get some rest. You've done exceptional work this week and I see no reason for you to stress yourself when you have a big job ahead of you."

"Big job. Right. Thanks." Junsu bowed his head slightly. Once he righted himself, he pressed the elevator call button and the doors slid open. He stepped past the threshold and turned around. Just before the doors closed, he stared out at his mother.

"I'm getting mated."

"That you are."

The elevator doors closed on Xijuan's Cheshire cat grin.

*

Sunday night rolled around. Before Junsu knew it, the city's once prismatic evening lights twisted and morphed into garish neon signs all reading THE END IS NIGH. He was being dramatic, obviously. This wasn't the end of his life in general, not by any means, but it was definitely the end of life as he knew it, the end of life as it had been before. The freedom of bachelorhood was being torn away from him and he was about to begin tumbling into the uncertainty of an arranged mating.

Already staring at the bottom of his third bottle of cider, Junsu lamented all of this to his friends that evening. He was sitting between Shik and Jaemin, siblings he had worked with since they'd started in the business, years ago, back when all three of them were in their twenties. And then there was Hong, Junsu's closest confidant and top soldier. She sat across the table with a sympathetic expression in place.

The four of them were enjoying a few drinks at a laid-back lounge in the eastern part of the entertainment district. The tiny bar was called The Red Lantern and it sat on a nicer part of the docks, overlooking the water. The moon was pale against a deep-blue sky. It was still pretty early in the night and they were all a bit tipsy, but Junsu was really bringing the mood down.

"Jeez, Jun. I know Xijuan but didn't think she could be so heartless. And with her own son," Jaemin teased, nudging Junsu in one shoulder. "I hope you like this Omega. Whoever he is."

"I've heard of Kaito Yamaguchi," Hong added in her usual somber tone. "He's the pride of that family...and I've heard he's a babe. He used to model for some magazine that's really popular with the Omegas in the Second Continent, you know. You could do worse, boss."

Junsu heard all of this, but he didn't take any of it in. His only response was to sigh and rub his palms over his tired eyes. He'd taken a picture of that vintage-looking photograph with his phone and showed it to all of them. The rumors were definitely true, Kaito was a beautiful young Omega, but that didn't make the situation any less jarring.

"I just wish I had more time," Junsu muttered. "This was sprung on me like a fucking trap."

"What do you need more time for?" Shik asked with a smirk. "To prepare for a having a mate or to fuck around?"

Junsu's only response was to groan because hell if he knew what he wanted. He slumped over the table, reaching for his fourth bottle. As he pulled himself back up, he took a nice long swig.

"Hey!" Junsu exhaled and slammed the bottle down onto the table. "What are you guys doing over the next two weeks? Are you busy?"

"Oh, no," Hong laughed. "No. No. No. You are not roping me into anything! I have an Omega of my own I'd actually like to see sometime. This job takes up enough of my day as it is."

Junsu huffed. He tended to forget, but Hong had gotten married a few months back. Her Omega was a businesswoman from the Northern Empire. They'd met one afternoon when Junsu had brought Hong along to work on the peace deals. At the time it had been adorable, but now it was an inconvenience.

"Fair enough," Junsu muttered before turning to the twins.

They had no defense against his big black eyes and that drunken pout pressing out his bottom lip. After being friends for years, they were used to seeing their boss drunk, but not like this. Junsu wasn't the type to pout. When Junsu wanted things done, he usually demanded it with a dark glare and a snap of his fingers.

This was different. He was clearly way out of his depths.

Jaemin was the first to relent with a heavy sigh. "All right!" he muttered. "You don't have to give us that stupid face. I get it."

"You'll come as my security detail," Junsu said with a grin, his mood lightening. "Apparently, my mother promised his family we could provide protection, so they don't have to send anyone across with Kaito."

"That's trusting," Hong commented with a nasally huff of a laugh. "But also, it's a fucking cruise. I'm sure it won't be a tough job, even for these two." She nodded at the twins with a smirk.

Jaemin pointedly ignored the jab. "Well, if anything happens to him, we'll have the entire Second Continent raining down hell on this city," he said with a wince. "So yeah, tough job."

After chugging back one more beer, Shik let out a loud, refreshed exhale.

"Sure! Why the fuck not? Let's go!" they declared. "Like Hong said, it's a fucking cruise. What possible security risks are there gonna be besides your new Omega seeing your ugly mug and needing to be rescued after he jumps overboard?"

They all laughed, even Junsu.

"Yeah, yeah," Junsu muttered.

They settled on that. Junsu did keep trying to convince Hong to come along as well, but she adamantly declined the offer even after he invited her Omega to come with.

"She hates boats," Hong replied. "She's literally never left the island because of it. No. I'll meet you guys at the docks with Xijuan Sun when you arrive back." With that decided, Hong lifted a glass as the night rounded itself off with a few cups of rice wine. That's when they really started drowning out the world.

"A toast! To Junsu and his Omega-to-be! May the awkwardness wear off eventually!"

"Cheers!" The other Alphas chimed in.

They clinked glasses and downed their shots.

"Get me completely hammered, you guys," Junsu said as the waiter came by with another round. The night was still young, and he was looking to forget his troubles.

*

Junsu vaguely regretted such a big bash on his last night of freedom, but it was worth it. Monday morning came after barely two hours of poor-quality sleep and he woke up nursing a massive hangover. He couldn't remember ever drinking so much in his entire life. It was a wonder he was still alive enough to get out of bed when the doorbell rang. He almost ignored it, but Noon was rubbing against his face and meowing at him for breakfast.

"All right, all right," he groaned, rolling off his mattress. He slept naked and so pulled on a silk robe before heading downstairs to answer the door. Through the morphed glass, he could make out a trim figure wearing a sleek black suit.

"Morning, Alpha Sun," the driver said in greeting as he opened the door. She tipped her hat and eyed his state of dress with a cheeky grin. "Vanna Tran. Your mother sent me. Your cruise departs in two hours from the South-West Commercial Port."

"Uh huh." Junsu looked her up and down while she did the same to him. With a resigned sigh, he eventually opened the door wide and walked away, allowing Vanna inside to wait while he got ready.

Vanna followed him, closing the door behind her. She whistled, and Junsu turned to see her eyeing his home with unhidden awe.

"Nice place you've got here. I think I saw it in a magazine once. Didn't you give some exclusive tour or something a few years back?" she asked.

"Yeah. Southern Interiors or something like that," Junsu replied as he turned on the espresso machine. He was a tea man, but desperate times called for desperate measures. "Can I get you anything? I just gotta feed the cat and shower, but you can take my bags, they're packed in the hall over there."

"Water would be nice. And no rush." Vanna smiled. "Like I said, the cruise departs in two hours. Should only take us a quarter of that to get through traffic."

"Great," Junsu replied automatically. He poured Vanna a glass before turning back to the sink and downing one himself. His head was throbbing, and the good morning small talk was killing him, but Vanna didn't let up. This was exactly why Junsu usually drove himself. These chauffeurs his mother hired were always way too bright and cheery in the ungodly hours of the morning.

"Your mother mentioned that you were picking up your mate from the Second Continent, taking him on a special cruise back," Vanna spoke with unhidden curiosity. "I didn't know you were engaged."

"Neither did I until a few days ago," Junsu grunted as he pulled the lid off a tin of cat food.

"Wait." Vanna raised a brow. "So, it's an arranged mating then?"

"Yeah," Junsu replied with a shrug. He would let the details remain vague—his mother would have made an announcement if she thought it pertinent—but he had a feeling she wanted to surprise the city with some big event. He cringed, thinking about the fanfare that would be waiting for him when he disembarked the cruise back with his new mate. Xijuan loved making headlines and Junsu imagined she'd been getting rather jealous seeing the announcements about the leaders of the North and Center.

"It's basically just business," Junsu muttered. "My mother is sick of seeing Dominik Wesa and Jimena Faraji hogging the tabloid headlines with all the news about them and their mates, so she's forcing me to get mated too."

"Well, if it's just business, I guess you wouldn't feel bad about having a little more fun before it's all official?" Vanna teased in a flirtatious tone. "What's one last little taste of freedom, hm?"

Junsu looked up at her and she winked, forcing a thoughtful "Huh" out of him. Normally, he would jump on that opportunity. Vanna was a good-looking Beta woman who would clearly be down for a quickie on the couch before Junsu got shipped off to meet his fate four thousand miles away.

Today, though, with a pounding headache and alcohol probably still coursing through his system, he just chuckled and shook his head.

"I'd take you up on it, but I think my new mate's family would probably have you killed."

Vanna cocked her head to one side, more curious than scared.

"What family?"

"Big one. Second Continent." Junsu spilled the information, knowing Vanna wouldn't be stupid enough to spread rumors at this point if she could hazard a guess who exactly he was talking about.

Silence hung like a chill in the air. Vanna stared at him before she finished her water off without another word. With a heavy exhale, she set down the empty glass and slid it toward Junsu.

"I'll see to your bags, Alpha Sun," she said, becoming rigidly formal as she stood. "Meet you on the driveway as soon as you're ready. Please, don't make me come knocking again."

"I'll try my best." Junsu smiled as he watched her go, only tearing his gaze away when she slipped into the hall to get his suitcases. He shook his head with a regretful sigh before sipping the last of his espresso and heading up to shower.

When he was washed, dressed, and ready to go, Junsu said goodbye to Noon, slipped on a pair of shades, and walked out into the morning light. Despite the tinted glasses the sun hit him like a floodlight, drawing out a groan.

"Ready to go?" Vanna asked cheerily, tossing away a cigarette as he turned from locking up.

"Yeah," Junsu replied. "Do you know who's coming to take care of the cat?" He gestured with a thumb in the direction of the house where he didn't have to look to see that Noon was watching him leave like she did every day, her face pressed up against the window, her sad mewling muffled by the glass.

Vanna chuckled. "Yes, your mother said she'd take on that responsibility personally. I'll be back here with Xijuan this afternoon."

"Great." Junsu nodded. Without another word he hopped into the back seat and let his head loll against the rest. He closed his eyes, tuning out the world for the duration of the drive.

Three: A Zen Cruise

The Zen Cruise Liner was one of the most luxurious ships on the market. The route it took between the Southern Empire's South-West Commercial Harbor and the Port of the Eastern Capital in the Second Continent was immensely popular, even though the views were purely oceanic and void of any scenery apart from the occasional sea life bobbing along the blue abyss. The ship itself lent to the Zen atmosphere and the name was no misnomer. Every piece of the extravagant vessel was designed to lend itself to a sense of relaxation and calm.

It was a massive boat, but extremely exclusive, the kind of cruise where there were at most one hundred people on board and nearly half of those people were staff and crew. A butler waited on the guests in each room and the chefs could prepare any number of dishes when they weren't making the exquisite meals and buffets that filled the banquet halls. The rooms were large and expansive, filled with luxury furniture and draped in fine fabrics. A spa on one of the floors had rooms emulating hot springs like in the bathhouses that were famous on the Southern Continent's big islands, where Kaito was from.

Junsu had been reading up on his Omega's homeland, trying to get to know him better before they met. It was hard finding anything about Kaito or the rest of the Yamaguchi family for that matter. They were extremely private and did not like appearing in articles and headlines the way the families in Luxor strived to.

Junsu ended up in the ship's spa for the entire first day while he was getting over his hangover. He took full advantage: mani, pedi, facial, sauna, the works. He even got Jaemin and Shik in on it because why the fuck not?

The week passed quicker than he would have liked. Part of Junsu was actually glad they were coming back because the facilities onboard were fabulous and he hadn't quite gotten the chance to sample them all. From the luxury dinners to the infinity pools stretching out over the ocean, the Zen Cruise really did have it all.

This wasn't Junsu's first time travelling to the Second Continent, but he'd never taken the cruise before. He knew his mother took it nearly every chance she got when visiting the Second Continent. She preferred the luxury of a cruise to the faster private transport ships Junsu usually took. Without a doubt, that was how she got the idea to send Junsu and Kaito out on what she clearly hoped would be a romantic getting-to-know-you trip before their bonding ceremony.

Junsu shuddered at the thought of the bonding ceremony and the awkward mating that would follow it. Maybe they wouldn't have to mate right away. Maybe Kaito would be happy to sleep in his spare room for a bit while they got used to each other. Maybe they could wait until Kaito was in heat, then neither of them would be thinking about how awkward and contrived their entire relationship was.

With a soft hum, Junsu stared at the photo of Kaito he still had saved on his phone. How would Kaito be as a mate? How would he be during heat? Shy or open? Prudish or keen? Junsu hoped they were a match. He'd heard that some Alpha and Omega pairs were literally incompatible. Would their scents mingle? Would they be repulsed by each other?

A heavy knock at the door shook him from his thoughts. He got up from where he'd been sipping tea on the balcony to answer it.

"Hey!" The burst of sound greeted him from Shik and Jaemin as soon as he opened the door. It was way too loud for first thing in the morning.

"Having a good time, Junsu? Feeling Zen?" Shik tittered.

"Welcome to your last day as a free Alpha!" Jaemin teased.

Junsu groaned. They'd had another rough night out at one of the bars on the upper deck, though they didn't go anywhere near as hard as they had back in Luxor. Still, all things considered, Junsu was feeling a little off that morning.

He managed to get dressed and follow the siblings down to the dining room. The chefs were serving a savory breakfast of rice, fish, and soup. It was different from the breakfasts they usually had back home. Even in the Southern Empire where most of the population had Second Continent ancestry, they tended toward a lot more of the typical New American cuisine. Breakfast was either sweet, pancakes and crepes, or it was eggs, bacon, sausage, and toast. On this cruise line, however, they catered more to the appetites of their Second Continent clientele.

Junsu was about to enjoy a bit of grilled salmon with a side of rice when Jaemin perked up.

"So, what's the plan today, boss?" he asked, words slightly muffled as he wiped his face with a napkin.

"We dock around noon." Junsu shrugged. "We should go into town for a bit, but we need to be back to meet Kaito before we cast off at six."

"Are we gonna wait at the top of the stairs for him like a prince and his knights?" Jaemin chuckled.

As Junsu lowered his face into the palm of one hand, Shik nudged their brother in the side with one elbow.

"Come on, man," Shik hissed, despite being responsible for a fair share of the teasing only moments before.

Jaemin pressed the back of his hand to his forehead and leaned into his sibling's side. "Alas, poor Junsu."

Junsu shook his head, trying his best to ignore Jaemin. They finished up breakfast and headed over to the patios at the head of the ship to catch their first glimpse of land in a week.

As they came into the Port of the Eastern Capital, rolling hills filled the western horizon. The Second Continent was a beautiful mix of city and nature. On the outer edge of the dense metropolis, many parts of the once expanding ports had been abandoned. The old buildings stood vast and empty, taken over by the twisting vines of nature. Ancient ruins left behind by the former denizens were an attraction for the real tourists aboard who were pulling out their phones and cameras to take pictures.

"All right, so like you said before, we have a few hours to go around town while they clean and restock the ship," Jaemin said as soon as they pulled into the harbor. He clapped his hands together, rubbing them excitedly as the ramps came down and they were given the signal to disembark. "Where do you guys want to start?"

Junsu was determined to truly relish his last few hours as a free man. Jaemin and Shik felt his pain, but Junsu was glad they'd opted to hold back their complaints. They clearly weren't too excited about being on Omega-watch duty for an entire week, but that minor annoyance didn't compare to what Junsu was going through. Hell, he'd be on Omega-watch duty for the rest of his life after marrying a high-profile figure like Kaito Yamaguchi.

With Jaemin and Shik flanking him all the way, Junsu explored the expansive covered market streets of the Eastern Capital. The entire district was a huge tourist trap, but the three of them couldn't have cared less.

The food was great. There was fresh fish just how they liked it in the South. The drinks were top quality; the kind of stuff they'd pay big bucks to import back home cost next to nothing in little kiosks scattered throughout the streets between the market stalls and back-alley sit-down restaurants.

There was so much to see in the Eastern Capital. And it was so full of tradition, things they'd heard about from elderly relatives back in the Southern Empire, but never really experienced. The city seemed as if it had hardly changed in a thousand years. Jaemin and Shik were like kids in a candy shop. At one point, they came by a souvenir store and decided to pick up a few snack foods they knew Hong would like. She'd probably murder them if they didn't bring something back despite her objections about joining them. The little trinkets and souvenirs were things you definitely couldn't get back in Luxor without coughing up way more cash than they were worth.

By the time their great adventure came to an end, they were all tuckered out. They sat on a stone bench under an old, red-painted arch surrounded by shopping bags. The three Alphas were quite a sight in their custom suits and sunglasses, gangsters on a shopping spree. Junsu swore he saw a group of giggling young girls in their school uniforms snapping a photo of them.

It was about a half hour until six o'clock when the ship would be casting off and heading back to Luxor City. Besides most of the staff and the crew, Junsu, Shik, and Jaemin were the only three who would be taking the same boat back. They walked up the gangway and stood at the railing, watching the new set of embarking passengers pass them by while they waited for Kaito Yamaguchi to make his appearance.

"Will he be able to recognize us, boss?" Jaemin asked. His sibling cocked their head to one side and they both glanced at Junsu with identical looks of curiosity.

"Yeah. At least I'm pretty sure he will," Junsu drawled. "They sent my mother an actual print photograph of him. I'm sure she sent them one of me in return."

"Were you all dressed up in nice traditional robes too?" Jaemin teased. "I'm sure he's picturing a prince in fine silks."

Again, Shik elbowed their brother in the ribs.

"If your mom didn't send over a picture, I'm sure Kaito would have looked you up," Shik said. "Once his parents told him he was marrying you, he must have gone online to check you out. I mean, I would have."

Junsu nodded, but his jaw clenched. *God damn it*, he wished his mother had told him sooner. Despite never having met Kaito, he'd met other members of the

Yamaguchi family before, brothers and cousins. So, someone in the family knew Junsu at least vaguely, but had anyone sent a picture to Kaito like the one he'd got?

He gritted his teeth at the thought. What if it wasn't a good picture? *Damn it.* Junsu knew he usually looked stern and could come off a bit cold, but not with his friends, and never with lovers. He didn't want his soon-to-be-Omega coming into this with any sort of daunting impression of who he was behind closed doors.

"Do you think he'll show up in full traditional gear like in that photo?" Jaemin asked, still teasing despite earning himself a fair number of warnings from Shik. "Think he'll be some kind of conservative prude?"

Junsu frowned at that, not sure if he should take offence and defend the honor of an Omega he had yet to meet, or if he should seriously consider the question because, *fuck*, maybe they *would* be sleeping in separate beds.

"Don't know," Junsu answered. "But I wouldn't call him a prude just because of that photo. It wasn't too bad. He just seemed...demure."

Shik agreed with him, casting a supportive smile before casting a glare at their brother who only smirked and shrugged in response.

The crowd started to thin out about ten minutes before they were due to cast off. It seemed to Junsu that everyone who was going to board had now boarded, but here he was, still standing at the top of the gangplank railing waiting for his future Omega. An uneasy feeling settled over him. He wondered if he'd just missed the young man coming in or—and this was the thought he felt most ambivalent about—maybe Kaito Yamaguchi wasn't coming at all.

But no.

Finally, about five minutes before they were way past due to leave, and a good ten minutes past the time when the last passengers were supposed to be allowed to board, a white luxury town car pulled right up to the base of the gangway, having somehow gotten permission to drive past the pedestrian only walkways.

All four car doors opened in unison and as expected, Kaito Yamaguchi and his entourage stepped out. The Omega slammed his car door, walked out onto the pavement, and immediately started making his way up the gangplank. They knew he was Kaito Yamaguchi because who else could he be?

The young man strutting toward them was a shocker. He looked...absolutely nothing like his photograph.

"What was that word you used earlier, Junsu?" Shik whispered as the Omega approached. "Demure?"

"He sure don't look demure, boss," Jaemin quipped.

Junsu could only stare, wide eyed and somehow managing to keep open mouthed out of the equation as he clenched his teeth and focused his control on his heavy jaw, just begging to drop.

The young man making his way up to the deck was miles apart from the traditionally robed Omega with slicked back hair Junsu had imagined he'd be greeting. Gone were all the traditional hallmarks of shy Omegan conservatism. Whoever was in that picture, Kaito Yamaguchi was clearly not trying to be that Omega.

The violet traditional robes that had covered every inch of Kaito's skin had hidden a lot. Now dressed all in white, Kaito would have looked heavenly, angelic even, if it weren't for the tattoos, and boy were there a lot of tattoos.

Junsu was speechless as he gave his future Omega a good long once-over.

Kaito was in a white button-down T-shirt, matching white shorts, and boat shoes. Beneath the hem of his shorts, and clearly visible peeking out from the spread of his half-unbuttoned shirt, intricately inked designs in all shades of purple and pink snaked their way over a smooth expanse of what would have been silk-white skin. Amethyst-colored flower petals danced down his arms on violet streams of water. Cherry blossoms bloomed lush and pink on branches that roped across his neck and shoulders. Some kind of water dragon weaved between waves and traced disturbed ripples through the stream all the way down to Kaito's delicate seeming fingers wrapped around an e-cigarette.

The Omega pressed the device to his rounded red lips and took a puff.

One design traced between Kaito's pectorals where an otherwise palm-wide strip seemed to be empty all the way down his torso. This single element was inked into a necklace-like design with large periwinkle beads. In the center of the lowest bead was a large ring and in the middle of that ring a single orthographic character was written in strong calligraphy.

Junsu recognized its meaning.

Kai. Ocean.

Junsu had to admit Kaito Yamaguchi was absolutely stunning. The picture, as nice as it was, really hadn't done him justice. Hell, Junsu would even go so far as to say the young man he was seeing in front of him now was much more exciting than what he'd imagined.

Not a demure little prude after all. Junsu wanted so badly to shoot a smirk back at Jaemin, but now was not the time.

Kaito stepped onto the deck, breathing a cloud of sweet-smelling pink smoke their way. He seemed to realize they were there to greet him. Why else would three overly formal-looking men be standing in formation just a few feet away from the gangplank? But Kaito just stared at them and didn't say hello.

A few steps behind Kaito, a clatter of sound drew their attention. Kaito spun around just in time to see the man carrying his cases up the gangplank had allowed one box to unceremoniously tumble to the ground as it slipped off the top of the pile he'd stacked it on.

While everyone else was watching the clumsy chauffeur, Junsu still only had eyes for Kaito. As he looked back, the turn of his shoulders had put his delicate neck on display. Junsu had been waiting to see that neck. It had been all concealed in Kaito's photograph, now it was all covered up with the last cherry blossom tendrils of his elaborate full-body tattoos. The things were everywhere. Kaito was literally inked from wrist to wrist and chin to ankles.

Junsu could hear a snort from Jaemin as another suitcase clattered to the ground. Kaito's man was crouched down struggling to pick up the first one while balancing the others and it wasn't exactly going very well for him.

"Um, excuse me?" Kaito snapped at his escort who was now breaking out in a sweat as he reached for the two fallen cases. "Are you serious? What the fuck are you doing? Do you have no respect for my things?"

The chauffeur managed to collect himself in a hurry. He contorted into a less ridiculous pose to pick up the cases. He then rushed up the gangway and stacked them neatly on the floor of the deck. As soon as he was finished, he turned to Kaito and bowed at the waist, holding his head low for a long while.

"Please forgive me, Omega Yamaguchi."

There was an ominously silent pause. Kaito sneered around his e-cigarette. "Just be careful with my shit. God! You're all so fucking lucky I'm leaving and don't have to see you again." He continued berating everyone who'd helped him from the car as they continued begging for forgiveness.

Once he was done, Kaito turned back to Junsu, Jaemin, and Shik. He eyed the three of them warily before sauntering up to Junsu.

Junsu raised a brow as Kaito approached, flanked by his poor abused escorts. The young Omega stepped right up to him, barely an inch away, and breathed a smoky breath into his face.

"You're the bodyguards, right? I was told there'd be bodyguards or some shit. If not, who the hell are you and why are you standing around like idiots?"

Junsu stared down at this rude little Omega. He somehow managed to hide his disbelief, but then a thought crossed his mind.

Kaito didn't recognize him.

"Sure," Junsu said abruptly, surprising Jaemin and Shik. "We're the bodyguards sent by Xijuan Sun to escort you to Luxor City's Southern Empire. Welcome aboard, Omega Yamaguchi."

"Great, then I'm sending these fuckwits home." Kaito snapped his fingers twice and his entire entourage bowed before walking off the boat. They got down to their car but waited to drive away. Kaito looked over one shoulder and noticed this with a huff. Junsu assumed they were probably just waiting to make sure he didn't try to jump ship.

"Ugh. Whatever." Kaito turned back to Junsu. "Okay, so who are—?"

Cutting him off with the sudden thrust of an extended hand, Junsu smirked and said, "It's a pleasure to meet you, Omega Yamaguchi. I'm Jaemin Yi."

Four: Playing Pretend

The real Jaemin Yi coughed suddenly as if he'd choked on a breath and Shik had to bite their tongue to keep from laughing out loud. The petulant Omega, Kaito, didn't seem to notice a thing.

"All right, whatever." Kaito didn't move to shake Junsu's hand; he simply walked past the three of them with a dismissive wave. "Can one of you take care of those?" he said with a sour expression as he gestured to his bags. He worded it as a question, but it wasn't so much a request as an order.

"Of course." Junsu snapped his fingers and the twins jumped to the task. They were both hiding their confused smiles behind piles of luggage as they trailed behind Junsu and Kaito.

"I guess I know who's boss here." Kaito huffed out an amused laugh. "I'm glad the Sun family sent hired help. Personally, I never trust the staff on these boats. You honestly never know who's going to try to pinch something." He said this out loud without seeming to care that the hall they were walking through was filled with said staff all milling about between room cleanings.

Junsu offered a sympathetic smile to a young cleaning woman who had clearly overheard if the disgust on her face was signal enough. She scoffed at his smile and turned away.

Junsu cringed. Well, he certainly wouldn't be expecting any chocolate on his pillow that night.

This is a good start. He shook his head. He, Shik, and Jaemin followed Kaito to his room where a butler waited outside. The tall and willowy Beta man bowed low, immediately recognizing his guest.

"Omega Yamaguchi," he said softly as he righted himself. "It will be my honor to serve you over the course of this—"

"Yeah, no," Kaito cut in. He lowered the sunglasses he was wearing and cast a look up and down the line of his butler's penguin suit. "I'm not down with this whole fancy personal butler thing. Get out of my face and don't bother me unless I call." With that said, Kaito snapped his fingers and held his palm out flat.

The butler's eyes widened. He cast Junsu a concerned glance before quickly producing the room key and handing it to his guest. He opened the door, letting Kaito and the others inside. Not one minute later they were pushed out and the door slammed shut leaving the butler, Junsu, and the twins standing in the hall looking shell-shocked.

"Jun—" the butler started only to be cut short when Junsu gestured quickly with a finger drawn across his throat.

"Come on," he whispered. All four of them left their rude little guest in his room and rushed away down to the other end of the ship's long hall.

"What the actual fuck was that?" the butler hissed, changing his tune as soon as they reached their destination. He pulled out a cigarette and lit up. After taking a long drag, he let out a breath but was clearly still rattled. "Your mother said he was a soft little thing. She warned *me* to be sensitive around *him*! Kid's a fucking demon."

Junsu patted the butler on the shoulder. Zhang Kim was a Beta and an old friend of the Sun family. He had been personally selected by Alpha Xijuan Sun to serve as Kaito Yamaguchi's butler on the cruise. Zhang was the head butler aboard a ship full of some of the best educated, highest quality hospitality workers in the world. And yet here he was, standing in an alcove in a back hall practically hiding from the young man he was meant to be looking after.

"Well, he's really something," Shik said in their usual supportive manner.

Junsu only dropped his head back against the metal wall of the ship with a low *thunk*.

"Why did you tell him you were *me*?" Jaemin all but shrieked. "What am I supposed to do now? Tell him I'm you?"

Zhang looked between Jaemin and Junsu, his cigarette burning away between his fingers. After a moment of silence, he let out a barking laugh.

"Oh my god, that's fucking hilarious," he uttered before taking another drag. He waved his cigarette at them. "You're pretending to be Jaemin? Why?"

"Yeah, Junsu Sun?" Jaemin replied, enunciating his real name pointedly. "Why *are* you pretending to be me?"

"I don't know!" Junsu snapped. "He was just being so...whatever you'd call that!" He gestured to Kaito's room with an exasperated sigh.

"What *do* you call that?" Zhang muttered.

"Junsu's future," Jaemin tittered.

"See, this is why I did it!" Junsu cut in as his friends sniggered at his expense. "I wanted you to take on a bit of my pain for once."

"Well, it's gonna work. Gonna piss me off this whole trip!" Jaemin snorted out a laugh.

"I'm going to tell the rest of the staff, this will be hilarious," Zhang said. "I imagine this boy would be acting a lot different if he knew it was his future Alpha he was shitting on."

Junsu huffed out a laugh, but he had to agree, it would be kind of hilarious to reveal himself at the end of the week. That would probably shock some sense into the bratty Omega he was soon to be mated to.

"Okay, tell the rest of the staff," Junsu agreed with a little smirk. "Don't let anyone let it slip that Junsu Sun is on board. We're just hired help. Bodyguards, like he said."

"But what about me!" Jaemin whined. His sibling caught him in a headlock and ruffled his hair.

"Oh, just go by the same name," Shik said. "Jaemin and Jaemin. It's not like that's never happened before."

Jaemin didn't like that idea. He muttered something to himself before snapping his fingers. "I'll go by Shik," he announced.

"God damn it…"

The twins argued for a while before Jaemin finally decided to go by Hong, since she wasn't there to complain. By the time he'd made this decision, the door down the hall had opened again and Kaito was just stepping out.

Zhang caught a glimpse of him and hid with Shik while Jaemin shoved Junsu into the hall.

"What the—? Really, guys?"

"You!"

Junsu straightened up and looked down the hall just in time to see Kaito marching toward him.

"It was a long drive to this stupid boat," Kaito snapped. "I'm starving! Where's the buffet? Take me."

"Ah, this way, Omega Yamaguchi," Junsu said with a gesture and a formal bow. As Kaito went on ahead of him, he turned to see his false friends giving him a thumbs-up from their secret corner.

Junsu gritted his teeth and turned away from them.

"Traitors," he hissed under his breath.

*

The cruise liner made its way back to Luxor City, beginning its weeklong journey home.

Junsu followed along behind Kaito as they walked along the ship's outer decks. He kept his gaze anywhere but on the sway of the tall Omega's hips. Annoying as he was, Kaito Yamaguchi had an allure about him that Junsu had to force himself to keep his eyes off. He shoved his hands deep in his pockets and muttered directions when appropriate.

"Follow me, Omega Yamaguchi," he said, dutifully pointing to the banquet halls.

Even these helpful interruptions seemed to irk Kaito. He huffed and turned on a heel, practically stomping his feet whenever Junsu told him what to do. Maybe he was just upset about this whole arranged bonding thing. Junsu wanted to ask but he didn't know how to do it without giving himself away.

So, he shrugged it off and continued to play the new bodyguard role he'd created for himself.

He shadowed Kaito into the ship's brightly lit dining room. It was located at the front of the lower deck where windows on all sides allowed the hall to be filled with light. The sea-blue roof refracted down beneath their feet as they stepped across a polished pale jade-green floor that resembled the ocean with its mix of colors and light.

Three times a day, the dining room offered full table service and the rest of the time there were a myriad of options to select from off a buffet table. The chefs were also on call to make specialty meals for any of the illustrious guests on board.

Kaito made a beeline for the buffet and immediately started loading up a large gold-trimmed plate. His innocent adoration of food made Junsu chuckle a little. He walked after the young man and started doing the same.

"What are you doing?" Kaito asked when he noticed Junsu loading up a rice bowl.

Junsu raised a brow. "Uh, getting something to eat?"

"Huh," Kaito stared at him silently for a long while. "The help doesn't usually eat with me."

The help? Wow. Junsu shrugged and kept dishing pieces of fish into his bowl. "Yeah, well, bodyguards get hungry too," he retorted with a little smirk. "And besides, I'm supposed to be keeping an eye on you. It'd look weird if I was just sitting there watching you eat alone."

Kaito actually grimaced at that. He clearly hated the idea of eating in front of people. It was probably part of the reason he'd wanted to get food right away, as he would know no one else would be there. The presence of the buffet meant that the full dinner service was over and typically people ate dinner before boarding.

As they sat down together, Junsu started eating first without much ceremony. It had been a long day shopping and walking the streets of the Eastern Capital and he'd only managed to grab a few snacks from a food stall or two. Then after they got back, he'd stood out on the deck with Jaemin and Shik for nearly an hour waiting for Kaito. He was fucking starving. Playing pretend as *the help* wasn't going to stop him from eating, goddamn it.

With his own chopsticks hovering delicately over his food, Kaito watched Junsu chow down. One side of his nose curled up in a bit of a sneer while the man across from him ate like an animal. "You know, for the record, I don't want you or any of your guys following me around. I don't need bodyguards shadowing me everywhere."

Junsu frowned and was about to protest, but Kaito stopped him before he could talk with his mouth full.

"Look, I just want to relax before my 'big day' and my mom pitched this trip to me as my last week of freedom, so after you're done stuffing your face, you can go, okay?"

Junsu stared at him with his next mouthful about an inch in front of his face. He paused like that for a moment and then popped the rice into his mouth and ate about five times slower than before.

Kaito groaned, but he clearly wasn't going to let some asshole bodyguard's antics spoil his appetite. With a narrow glare ever fixed on Junsu, he started eating as well.

"So," Junsu started, drawing out his meal even further by establishing a conversation between bites, "you're going to be mated to Junsu Sun. How do you feel about that?"

The fury that lit up Kaito's eyes was only matched by his appetite as exhibited by the fact he swallowed before lashing out.

"What are you trying to do? Strike up a fucking conversation?" he hissed.

Junsu bit his bottom lip to hide a smirk. "Junsu is...my boss. So, we're close. He's told me how he's feeling about all of this, I just wanted to see how you are. You know. To compare."

"Well," Kaito started as if he were going to go on a rant. And rant he did. "About a month ago my mother is pulling me into some artistic traditional shoot to get my photo taken, and I'm sitting there thinking it's for the family collection or something, but no. I'm in one of our fancy little gardens in this huge mess of fabric and that's when she tells me. Of course, my father isn't there, she knew I'd be able to sway him to my side. In the end she convinced me, but I'm still pissed she tricked me into that stupid photo. It's embarrassing! And not to mention the Sun family didn't send one."

Clearly, Junsu thought but said nothing.

Kaito sighed dramatically. "I guess I should have seen it coming. This is what they raised me for after all."

*

One month before the cruise.

Kaito Yamaguchi sat in front of one of the sliding wood doors of the family compound. Light from outside shone down onto the bamboo floor creating a picturesque scattering of mottled shadows. The door was half open and the blooming cherry blossom trees outside hung over a clear blue pond.

Despite the beauty of the garden right behind him, Kaito sat with his head turned away from the view, facing a large camera and staring into a glaring box light.

"Perfect, Omega Yamaguchi. Hold this pose if you would, please."

Kaito resisted rolling his eyes and did as he was asked. He only obeyed for so long, however. His gaze soon shifted over to where his mother stood.

Kazue Yamaguchi, the Alpha leader of the entire Second Continent, stood off to the side, just behind the photographer's setup. As usual, she was on her phone. Business. The empire never sleeps.

Slight and smooth skinned, Kazue appeared young for her age. She had dressed in a slim-cut suit that fit tight around her thighs and shoulders, a powerful look for a powerful woman.

Kaito huffed. He'd probably be wearing something like that if he wasn't stuck in the hundred layers of patterned fabric his mother had tricked him into.

"You still haven't told me what all this is for, Mother."

"Now, now, Kai." Kazue didn't even look up from her phone. "Smile for the camera. These photos are very important."

"But why? I told you before, I'm done modeling." Kai tutted as he turned his head toward the garden. "It's boring."

"Eyes forward, Kai. Also, these photos aren't for your modeling portfolio."

"Then what are they for?" Kai whined even as he turned back to the camera. The sullen look on his face was surely ruining the shoot.

With a sigh, his mother finished texting and hit send on the message. She inhaled deeply and cast a narrow gaze around the room. With a snap of her fingers the camera crew cleared out swiftly, leaving her alone with her son.

Kai's chest tightened and he grew nervous as his mother approached. She gracefully took up the seat the photographer had been in before. Her cold black eyes never left his.

"Kaito..."

*

That was when he'd first learned about the engagement. Kaito remembered the rage that had filled him. The injustice of it all. But he also understood his duty. *This was what he'd been raised for.* He knew that. Hell, he'd known as soon as his first heat hit and he was old enough to understand the difference between Alphas, Omegas, and Betas.

His mother had been fairly candid about her expectations. He would marry a good Alpha from a strong family. Her standards set on both those descriptors were sky high, so high in fact, Kai never thought he'd ever have to get mated.

And then Junsu Sun became the last eligible bachelor left in Luxor City. Damn him.

Shaking the memories away, Kaito slammed his chopsticks down on the table. "So now I'm the one with a stupid photo and I'm the one who has to make my way to my Alpha-to-be and I'm the one who has to be a good little Omega. So yeah, sorry not sorry that I'm a little fucking ticked off and this is going to be my last week to truly express that. Before..." Kaito stopped and sighed heavily. "I mean, I guess I knew this was coming, being the only Omega in the family and all. And I'm sure it'll be fine, but I just didn't picture things this way, you know?"

*

Junsu stared at him, holding a breath. Yes. He knew.

"So, your parents weren't exactly in agreement then? Sending you to Luxor?"

Kaito rolled his eyes and looked away. He sighed heavily and Junsu could see him deflate visibly as a kind of sulky sadness took over.

"No, well, yes. My Alpha mother is all for it, no qualms at all. Reputable family. Good for business. My Omega father doesn't like that I'm being sent away, but he didn't protest much. Really, I think he's just glad I'm finally getting mated." Kaito's features scrunched up as he put on a high-pitched voice Junsu could only assume was meant to be his father. "*He'll be a perfect match, Kaito. The Sun family is such a good one and you won't find a more suitable Alpha. Besides, you're not getting any younger. Beauty fades, you know*?" Kaito finished with a disgusted scoff.

Junsu's brow arched, but he kept his expression sympathetic yet composed when Kaito looked searchingly into his gaze.

The Omega's voice was surprisingly soft when he licked his lips and said, "Anyway, I don't know why I'm telling you all this. But you said you talked to Junsu Sun?" Kaito bit his lip. "About the arrangement? What did he say?"

Junsu looked into the Omega's eyes and saw something behind all the rage and fire. Deep down in those dark orbs, there was a hint of that demure Omega they'd joked about before. Kaito was scared…vulnerable.

And so, Junsu told the truth.

"Alpha Sun is nervous," Junsu started. "This has been hard on him. I—I honestly think he was sort of planning on being a lifelong bachelor, you know? He's a little on edge about the whole bonding thing, but everyone knows it's politics. Good for business. For both families, right? Like you said. Anyway, he's like you, I suppose. Hopeful that it'll be all right in the end, even if this whole arrangement has had a rocky start."

Junsu knew he was not anywhere near as eloquent as Kaito had been. The Omega could speak his mind and express himself with such ease, unfiltered, not caring if it came off as rude. Even though everything Junsu had said was the truth and, in his opinion, not too far off from how Kaito was feeling, the small huff the Omega let out told him it wasn't what he'd wanted to hear.

"Oh yeah, this arrangement must be *so* hard for Junsu Sun," Kaito muttered, stabbing into a piece of fish with one chopstick. "Having a mate from a good family shipped right to the doorstep of his shitty island city in the middle of the Pacific fucking nowhere. Must be so damn hard for him."

"Hey, now," Junsu said, getting defensive for himself even though he wasn't supposed to be himself at that moment. "I—He—Junsu's a great guy and—and Luxor's a pretty amazing place. You'll see once you get to know it. You've never been, right? You gotta at least give it a chance."

"Whatever. Now you really just sound like my mom." Kaito rolled his eyes. He tossed his chopsticks to the table next to his bowl and stood, not caring about the wasted food on his plate or if his chair screeched against the polished floor. "I'm going back to my room."

"Kai—" Junsu stopped himself from being too informal. Wiping his face quickly with a cloth napkin, he stood and followed Kaito out of the dining room. He was a few steps behind the Omega who didn't seem to have any trouble tracking in reverse to find his way back to his room.

Kaito disappeared around the wall just as they came to the final turn and Junsu followed only to find he had stopped not one foot away from the corner of the wall. He was turned to his oncoming stalker with a dark glare already in place.

"Oh my god! Stop following me!" Kaito all but screamed.

Junsu nearly jumped, but his features somehow remained a placid mask of indifference in spite of the onslaught. Kaito's face was hot, and he was sure it must be red with emotion, but if it was from being followed or from their conversation earlier, he couldn't tell.

"Did you not hear me before?" Kaito demanded. "I said, I don't need any of you assholes shadowing me this whole trip."

"Look, I don't like this any more than—" Before he could out himself, Junsu snapped his mouth shut. He'd almost revealed too much. Shaking his head, he took a breath and went on to simply reply, "I've been ordered to look after you."

"Well, I don't need you," Kaito spat. He stared Junsu down. "Now leave me alone before I call security."

With that said, Kaito turned on his heel and fled down the hall.

Junsu watched him leave, indignantly shaking his head. "I am security!" he shouted back.

Kaito only raised a middle finger before disappearing into his room.

Five: Another Luxor City Lover

"*Kaito*," Kenichi Yamaguchi drawled, his voice a singsong tenor. Kaito's oldest brother spoke in a deep, loose drone as he chastised him over the phone later that day. "You should not be so cruel to your poor bodyguards. You know, your Alpha sent those men to keep you safe during the journey."

"Future Alpha," Kaito corrected his brother snappily. "And what's there to keep me safe from?" He gestured around him even though he knew Kenichi couldn't see that he was laying under a modern brise-soleil, sprawled across a sunbed on the private patio with nothing for miles ahead but a clear ocean view. "It's a fucking luxury cruise! What's gonna happen? Am I gonna get relaxed to death? Or do you have some information about some rich-bitch Luxor City Omega on the boat plotting against me for stealing the last eligible bachelor on their shitty island?"

"*Kaito*." Again, his brother's disapproving drawl made him want to hang up, but he'd called Kenichi because he'd been feeling homesick after that horrible conversation with that idiot bodyguard. Kenichi was his eldest brother and the Alpha who would inherit after their mother passed on. He'd already started taking on duties across the Second Continent, but still always made time for Kaito. They were close and, of everyone in the family, Kenichi was the one Kaito would miss the most.

"I hate this. It hasn't even been one day yet! How am I going to survive?" Kaito whined, rubbing his face and trying to keep his emotions at bay.

"You'll live, baby brother. You know, I told you I've met Junsu before, remember? It was a few years back, last time I was in Luxor on business. He's a very calm and kind Alpha, despite this line of work we are all in. You'll see when you meet him. Even our father agrees, or he wouldn't have let you go."

Kaito groaned. He trusted his family, but that didn't mean he liked any of this. He felt as if his whole life was being steered for him. There was absolutely no way for him to reach the wheel to get back on track because the wheel was an ocean away in his mother's iron fist.

"I just wish I had more time," Kaito whispered more to himself than to Kenichi.

"No." His brother's response was immediate. "You are young, the best age for change, uprooting yourself, starting a new life. And you won't have your youth forever. The longer you wait, the harder these things get, you know?"

"Um, I don't need advice on my looks from a fortysomething-year-old Alpha, thanks. God, you sound like Dad. I'm hanging up," Kaito hissed. He pulled his phone away from his ear to do just that.

"Wait! Wait! Kaito, I just want to let you know I am very proud of you. We all are. This is a big change for you, but it will be a huge opportunity for our family ties."

Kaito stared out into the sea to watch the sunset on the horizon. The violet sky faded to orange. Far to the west it would still be light out where his brother was back home in the Eastern Capital. He was silent, hypnotized by the colors until Kenichi's questioning voice drew him back to reality.

"Kaito?"

"I know," he whispered. "I know. Thank you, Keni."

"No. Thank you, Kai. I love you!"

Kaito scoffed. He could practically hear the shit-eating grin in his brother's voice. He blew a raspberry into the mic before hanging up on the sound of his older brother's laughter.

He lay back on the sunbed, smiling to himself. Maybe this wouldn't be so bad. Maybe he'd get used to his new life, just like everyone kept telling him he would.

Maybe things would be all right.

*

The next morning, Kaito ordered breakfast to his room. He didn't want to eat alone in that big dining hall, and he especially didn't want to accidentally run into his bodyguards who he knew would be down there eating with the rest of the guests. After talking with his brother, he felt a little bit bad, especially for the head bodyguard he'd had dinner with the evening before. What was his name again? Oh right, *Jaemin*.

There was a knock at the door.

Kaito shook his head and answered it. His personal butler whose name tag read simply Zhang stood there with a tray, smiling cordially despite the telling-off Kaito had given him the evening before.

Kaito gestured for him to put the food on the table without saying a word of thanks, not that a butler should have been expecting anything of the sort.

Zhang bowed and was just about to go when Kaito's abrupt shout made him jump.

"Hey!" he called out, snapping his fingers at Zhang. "Where are those other guys?"

Zhang looked to the door as if making sure his escape was clear. "Ah, your bodyguards? They'll be around the ship somewhere."

Kaito shot him the angriest look upon receiving that obvious response. "Of course, they're around the ship somewhere, it's not like they hopped off to tour some uninhabited little island halfway through the night."

Zhang cleared his throat. "They're probably just enjoying the onboard facilities and entertainment since you sort of gave them the time off."

Kaito huffed because, yeah, he did technically tell them to go away, but now he was bored and alone.

"Could I get you anything else, Omega Yamaguchi?"

Kaito looked between Zhang and his breakfast.

"No, get out." He waved the butler off before getting up and tucking in to eat. He finished, watched some TV, took a bath, and even started reading a book before boredom finally overwhelmed him completely. With a strangled sigh, he got up, put on something apart from the fluffy bathrobe he'd been lounging about in all day, and left his room. It was about two o'clock and lunch would be served soon, but Kaito wasn't looking for food.

He wandered around the ship until he got to the sun deck on the upper level. An intricately designed canopy swirled over the center of the patio, shading the bar and seating area. Glass panels separated walkways that were split up by five long infinity pools stretching out over the sides of the ship. Decorative glass curved up to the sky. The ship must have looked like a lotus blooming from above.

Kaito walked down one of these aisles and through the seating area to the bar. It was pretty busy; a lot of Alphas were standing about, a few Omegas either on their arms or bathing in little groups in the fancy pools. Kaito supposed drinking was one of the favored activities on board these all-inclusive cruise lines.

He couldn't help rolling his eyes at the other Omegas wandering about. Of course, everyone else was wearing their most appealing bathing suits and light, flowing fabrics and here he was in a stiff white-and-purple patterned jinbei. He was probably richer than all of them put together, but he felt and looked like a great big child.

It didn't help that he could really go for the tallest pinkest drink on the menu. And strawberry flavored too? Yes, that was exactly what he needed.

Kaito ordered his beloved Strawberry Fizz from the overly smiley bartender. Seriously, the guy needed to go lighter on the charm and way heavier on the vodka.

He turned around and leaned back against the bar while he waited. It was annoying to see so many couples. Young or old, it didn't matter, they were all annoying Kaito. He threw his head back and sighed.

They weren't so bad. He wanted so desperately to believe they weren't so bad, but every time he watched some Omega send a loving glance their Alpha's way or some Alpha laughing at a joke his Omega had whispered into his ear, it just reminded him he wasn't ever going to have that. And it wasn't just because of this whole arrangement. No. Even before, Kaito had never been a sweet demure little Omega. He was taller than most, his mother always called him her supermodel. Hell, he'd even done a few photoshoots because of it. But out in the real world some Alphas considered him intimidating. Well, they weren't wrong, and he had a tall personality to match.

Impatient. Impassable. Impossible. He wasn't the type of Omega most Alphas were aiming to date, not that Kaito had ever been allowed to date. Because of his status, the family business had kept him in a pretty structured routine his entire life, but now here he was, given free reign for one week before his new family would chain him up all over again.

Kaito sighed.

The bartender purred something to get his attention. Kaito turned around to get his drink before spinning back, ignoring the man's obvious flirtation. He continued glowering at the couples lounging around the sundeck.

Sipping on a fresh pink strawberry cocktail, he glared into the room. People were now completely avoiding his side of the bar. He was purposely giving off a violent, seething aura. Not even bothering to hide the tattoos poking out through the sleeves and leg holes of his jinbei, Kaito made sure everyone knew who he was and where he came from.

He caught a few people staring at him, but they looked away as soon as they were seen. Little groups formed and their eyes flashed to him before they leaned together to whisper and murmur in carefully hushed tones.

Let them talk.

Then there was a shift. Eyes widened and people angled themselves toward the other end of the room. All of a sudden, Kaito Yamaguchi wasn't the most interesting thing to stare at anymore.

Intrigued by the turn of events, Kaito's gaze followed those of a few looky-loos, tracing their line of sight over to fall on a couple who'd just come in under the canopy past one of the glass panels. They strolled in, looking like they owned the place.

The Alpha was tall, tan, and handsome as a movie star fresh off a tropical island shoot. He had one arm wrapped around the waist of the gorgeous Omega at his side.

Kaito vaguely recognized them. He'd definitely seen the Alpha somewhere, in the news or on TV or something. He had to be a celebrity of some sort; there wasn't a single politician in the world sporting an undercut that sharp. And the Omega, well, he was simply perfect. Tiny, lithe, and positively glowing on his Alpha's arm.

Kaito watched with a jealous sneer as the utter specimen of an Alpha pulled his Omega to face him. The Omega looked up at his Alpha as the taller man leaned down to press a perfect little kiss to the perfect little lips of his perfect little Omega.

God, does he really have to be that much of a stereotype? The Omega was almost a full head shorter than his Alpha, standing on the tips of his toes to meet his mate's lips. He was so small and lean and disgustingly adorable in his crop top and high-waisted shorts.

Like really? Kaito mentally groaned. He couldn't help but pout when Little Mr. Perfect Omega slipped out of his Alpha's embrace and started making his way toward Kaito's side of the bar. A few people looked like they wanted to warn him to stay back, but they all turned away to avoid Kaito's glare.

Kaito turned, too, and ordered another drink. He was going to need it.

"Hey! That looks amazing!"

Kaito side-eyed the other Omega who'd started nattering away as soon as he arrived at the bar. The last thing he had been expecting was for anyone to strike up a conversation with him.

"What are you drinking?" Little Mr. Perfect Omega asked with a cheery smile that grated on Kaito like sandpaper.

"It's called a Strawberry Fizz," he muttered around his straw. "Careful, it's got vodka in it. We wouldn't want you tripping over your designer flip-flops."

As soon as the words left his mouth, Kaito realized how fucking petty he was being. He honestly usually wouldn't have given a damn, but when he cast a glance over to the now quiet Omega, he could see his dark brows knitting together into a shy expression.

The Omega blinked down at his shoes, looking a little embarrassed.

Kaito tried to shrug it off. For all he cared, Little Mr. Perfect Omega could go run on back to his impossibly hot Alpha and cry on his big broad shoulders.

He got a surprise though. The other Omega looked up at him again, and then his face broke out into a smile. Suddenly, he descended into a fit of giggles, slapping a hand on Kaito's shoulder and giving him a playful shove.

"You're terrible! I love it! What's your name?"

Kaito stared at him for a long while, before sputtering out, "I'm Kaito Yamaguchi. But—just Kai for short." He didn't know why he said it; only his family and closest friends called him Kai.

"Nice to meet you, Kai!" the other Omega replied. He held out the hand on which a black and gold bonding ring shone bright. "I'm Lin Vasi—oh! Sorry! Lin Wesa." He laughed. "You'd think after two years I'd be able to get used to that."

As Kai shook his hand, it took a second for the name to click into a recognizable place in his memory. When it did, he nearly choked on his drink.

"Lin Wesa?" *Holy shit*. Kai blinked rapidly. "You're Dominik Wesa's Omega? From the Central Empire in Luxor City?"

Lin blushed a little and shrugged his shoulders up to his ears. "That's me!" he said coyly. "It's so funny! Like I'm famous now or something."

"Or something," Kai laughed, putting it all together now. Dominik Wesa had made headlines twice in one year, first with the unification of the island capital and then again when he announced his bonding to some nobody Omega from New America, Lin Vasiliev. It was a big shock among the socialites from Luxor City to the Second Continent across the Golden Desert and all the way down to the Latin Independent, all of whom had their eyes set on Dom and his Empire. Any hope of a mating arrangement quashed, they all realized they'd have to go about doing business the old-fashioned way. There'd be no easy ins through a bond now.

Kai was pretty sure Dom and Lin Wesa's bonding was what first started the mess of an arranged mating he was now being faced with. His parents were obviously keen to scoop up the last available Alpha in Luxor City's leading families for their only Omega son. Anything less than the leader, or in this case the future leader, of an Empire would be wholly unacceptable.

In his own way, Lin was out of place here, just like him. Kai eyed Lin with a languid gaze, tracing him up and down as he sipped his drink. Strangely, he was feeling a new sense of kinship with Little Mr. Perfect Omega.

They both took a seat on a bar stool, facing each other with drinks in hand.

"So, what brought you two to the Eastern Capital?" Kai asked.

"Well, it was just business for Dom." Lin rolled his eyes for a moment before focusing a narrow stare at Kai. "You said your name is Yamaguchi? Any relation to Kenichi Yamaguchi?"

Kai nodded. "My oldest brother." Kenichi didn't usually talk business outside of his work hours. Kai wasn't surprised he hadn't heard about this little meeting.

"Oh! Okay, so you're that Kaito! I didn't want to assume anything. He mentioned you. Wow. Small world." Lin tittered. "Anyway, the cruise was a gift from Dom. The business trip overlapped with our two-year anniversary."

Kai laughed at Lin's little pout. "Business is business I suppose," he said with a shrug.

"I suppose," Lin huffed. He was still clearly getting used to the concept that Kaito had grown up his entire life around. Everything—life, friends, relationships, even family—had to be set aside for business at times.

"Anyway, so what are you doing here?" Lin asked, changing the subject. "Just enjoying a cruise? Are you planning an extended vacation in Luxor? You should come up to the Central Empire and visit! I'm sure Dom would be happy to host!"

"Actually," Kai drawled, pinching his bottom lip between his teeth, "the news isn't out yet, but I'm about to join the ranks of the Luxor City Lovers."

Kai couldn't help laughing at the little nickname the tabloids had given Lin Wesa and Atsadi Faraji, the two bond mates of Luxor City's once most eligible leaders, Dominik Wesa of the Central Empire and Jimena Faraji, the newly reinstated leader of the Northern Empire. On hearing it, Lin gasped knowingly, eyes wide and sparkling with a mixture of shock and excitement.

"No way!" he cried, clapping his hands. "So, you're Junsu Sun's Omega? I had no idea he was even seeing anyone!"

"Yup, I'm his mate-to-be," Kai replied with a half smile and a shrug. He looked away and stirred his drink absently. "It's no wonder you didn't know. Our parents arranged it about a month or so ago. Though I only found out two weeks back."

Lin's excited smile immediately turned into a frown. "Wait. Did you say 'arranged'?"

"Yup," Kai sighed. "You know, I literally haven't even seen a picture of him."

"No way!" Lin said again. It was starting to sound like his catchphrase.

Kai let out a huffing laugh. "Yes way," he replied with a sour tut. He stared straight ahead, taking a sip of his drink.

"You don't know what he looks like? That's ridiculous!" Lin said, agog. "I mean, you could look him up online."

"Meh," Kai huffed. "I don't wanna spoil the surprise. And honestly, I probably have seen a photo or two in magazines or in the news or something. If I'd known that was going to be my future Alpha, I might have paid more attention."

"Yeah, but I mean—" Lin pulled his phone out from god knows what pocket in those tiny shorts of his and started flipping through his pictures "—I feel like I might have a recent photo from the last dinner party we all went to."

Kai covered his eyes with one hand and waved Lin's phone away. "Don't show me any pictures! I just don't want to get my hopes up or anything like that."

"Why not?" Lin asked. His brow creased, clearly puzzled by the odd reaction. His phone hung limply in his palm.

"I don't know." Kai let out a heavy breath. "I just feel like you sort of create these strange versions of people in your mind based on their photos sometimes. No matter what, you'll always be either surprised or disappointed when you meet the real person. You know? Usually I wouldn't give a shit, but in this case, well, it's different."

"Totally," Lin drawled in reply. In his palm, he had a photo gallery open. The pictures in it looked like they had been taken at some fancy dinner party. Lin had scrolled to a picture of someone who must have been Junsu. Kai couldn't see his face clearly in his peripheral vision, but the Alpha was looking dapper in a maroon silk suit, smirking at something someone next to him was saying.

Kai turned away.

Lin's finger was hovering over the picture, obviously tempted to click and enlarge it so Kai could see, but he respected the other Omega's wishes and tucked his phone away. "I suppose you're right. I mean, I'd seen pictures of Dom before we'd ever met, and he always looked so serious in the news. I could have never guessed he'd turn out to be such a kind and...generous mate."

"Generous." Kai raised a brow and hummed around the rim of his drink. "Let's hope we're all so lucky."

"You have nothing to worry about with Junsu," Lin said, placing a supportive hand on Kai's arm. "He's perfectly charming."

"I trust you. I trust my family, too, of course," he said with a laugh. "But you've probably met Junsu more, know him better. So, is he nice? And attractive? In real life. Like..." Kai waved a hand in a vague gesture and his giddy brain stalled for a minute. "Give me a one to ten ranking of Junsu Sun on a bad day."

A slight blush covered Lin's cheeks in a flash of red. He laughed, and seemed to be trying to will it away, which was a good sign.

Kai thought back to stories he'd read about in the news that came out of Luxor City. Two years ago, the unification of the empires was splattered all over every headline of every tabloid, online and off. There had been a huge celebration at Xijuan Sun's club the evening when Junsu had come back to the Southern Empire after helping Dominik Wesa dismantle the Northern Leadership, reinstating Jimena Faraji as the Alpha leader in the North. Junsu Sun had often been described as fearsome and handsomely disheveled. There hadn't been any pictures from inside the private club, not that Kai remembered seeing, but Lin had to have first-hand knowledge of the night.

Still blushing, Lin bit his bottom lip. His gaze darted around the room and soon landed on his Alpha. Dom was speaking with a group of other Alphas out on the deck, so Lin leaned into Kai's side and whispered, "I shouldn't say, but Junsu is seriously up there. Don't tell anybody I said it, but he's like a nine out of ten at least."

Lin winked and Kai raised a brow.

"Nine at least, huh?" he chanced a quick glance over to Lin's Alpha. The man he now knew to be Dominik Wesa, the leader of Luxor City's Central Empire, was definitely the hottest man on deck. Dressed to impress, even on holiday, he wore chic aviators and a patterned T-shirt he'd only bothered to button halfway up his tan muscular chest. "Does that sit your Dominik at a ten then? Or does he break the meter?"

Kai couldn't help but smirk at Lin's reaction. Lin's pale cheeks darkened to their deepest red yet, but he smiled.

"I'm being serious," Lin said. "Junsu is a catch, and I'm sure you'll grow to like each other."

Kai turned back to his drink, sighing a little. He and Junsu probably would grow to like each other, Lin was right. But still, Kai had always hoped for more. He wanted that deep connection Omegas were so often told about, the sort of thing the tabloids and gossip columns gushed over in articles detailing Dom and Lin's chance romance or Jimena and Atsadi's star-crossed love.

Kai was so sure he'd find that one day. He'd always hoped it would just magically come to him. But now those hopes were gone. This whole arrangement had changed everything.

"Thanks, Lin," Kai breathed. He was a little disheartened, but still smiling. "I needed some reassurance."

"No problem!" Ever a ray of sunshine, Lin's smile brightened the dour mood. "For now, we should enjoy the cruise! Right? Oh! And you have to tell me about these tattoos! Just wow!"

Kai and Lin stayed at the bar together chatting. The subject ranged from tattoos to culture to where they both grew up. Kai learned a lot about Luxor from Lin, gaining insight into all the little tidbits about the city he'd be calling home soon enough.

Eventually Lin wanted to go for a swim and convinced Kai to come with him. Kai hadn't brought a bathing suit—hell, he didn't even own a bathing suit—so he just sat at the edge of the pool in his jinbei, shorts pulled up high, lower legs dipping into the water. He stared down at his feet, only looking up to talk with Lin every once in a while as he swam by.

They eventually parted ways but made sure to exchange numbers. Lin invited Kai to sit with him and Dom for a meal if he wanted and Kai tentatively accepted. He still didn't feel like eating in front of other people and he especially didn't want to risk a run-in with the bodyguards. Not after how he'd treated them.

As he strolled back to his room that afternoon, he thought about all the things Lin had told him about Junsu. He started feeling a little bad for the way he'd reacted to the men his future mate had sent to watch out for him. The guilt sort of pissed him off, but he didn't know how to change it. He'd said what he'd said and done what he'd done. He wasn't really sorry, but he wasn't proud of himself either.

With a heavy sigh, Kai stopped on the part of the deck that had a patio just before the hall leading to his room. He pulled his e-cigarette out of his pocket and started smoking. Leaning against the edge of the railing, he looked out at the pool deck below and the ocean beyond. After a long drag, he let out a smoky breath.

"You know, those things'll kill you."

Kai looked over to see the leader of his little troupe of Southern Empire bodyguards approaching. What was his name again? Jae-something?

He pressed his e-cig to sneering lips as the bodyguard swaggered over. Kai tried to ignore him, but he couldn't help casting a quick up and down glance over the line of his body. He didn't walk like any bodyguard Kai had back home; they were always either stiff and military or jittery and apprehensive. This man walked with his head held high and he always seemed to have a cocky smirk in place.

"It's a vape," Kai drawled in reply, turning away. "Worst I'll do is somehow drown myself in nicotine."

The bodyguard chuckled, drawing Kai's attention once more. He had a nice laugh and Kai couldn't help but find him attractive. Junsu Sun was clearly a man who liked to surround himself with good-looking people. His inner circle certainly wasn't lacking.

"What was your name again?" Kai asked.

The man stared at him for a calm pause and casually shoved his hands deep in the pockets of his pale-gray suit pants before answering, "Jaemin Yi."

"Right." Kai took another drag on his cigarette. "Jaemin, can you get someone to bring dinner up to my room?"

The bodyguard seemed surprised, but he replied, "Sure."

"Thanks."

"Of course, Omega Yamaguchi."

Kai glared at the man as he pressed a hand to his chest and bowed his head.

"Oh please. Stop that."

Still bowed low, his bodyguard glanced up at him. Kai noticed an amused little spark in his dark eyes. "What am I doing wrong now?"

Kai huffed. "You're being weird and formal because I yelled at you earlier. I'm not yelling anymore, so you can stop."

The bodyguard raised a brow and replied, "But I have no idea when you'll start yelling. I'm following you again, aren't I? Wasn't that what set you off before?"

Touché, Kai thought with a huff. "Well, I changed my mind. You were hired to follow me by my future Alpha, so you can follow me around if you're supposed to."

"Nothing would give me more pleasure."

A disgustingly charming smirk hid in the corner of the bodyguard's lips. A piece of Kai wanted to smack it off his smarmy face and another piece, well, that piece didn't matter. He resisted both urges.

"Look," Kai snapped. "I just don't want you getting in trouble with Junsu Sun because of me, okay? Do your job and try not to get in my way."

Kai didn't want to get himself in trouble either. Considering this Alpha bodyguard of his was apparently good friends with his Alpha-to-be, someone Junsu clearly considered a confidant, Kai was going to try to be polite...nice even.

It wouldn't be so hard, right? He'd be nice to Jaemin and Jaemin would report back to Junsu telling him how sweet his new Omega was. Then Junsu wouldn't be all nervous and they could try to start "growing to like each other" just as Lin said.

Kai nodded to himself. It was the perfect plan if he could just remember to be nice.

Be nice, Kai. Be nice.

Six: "Hey! You! Bodyguard!"

Junsu let out a low groan as the voice of his future Omega carried through the halls of the ship. Kai just couldn't bother to remember his stupid fake name. It was probably for the best—he'd have to come clean at some point, but it was too early in the morning to even think about that.

He ate a light breakfast on one of the semi-private canopies looking out behind the ship. On the way over, the area above the ship's rudder had always been quiet. People avoided it because the view mainly consisted of the ship's jutting backside. Junsu had started using it as his little piece of sanctuary. He wasn't exactly hiding, but he had no idea how Kai had found him.

It was the beginning of the third full day of their week-long cruise and while Kai had managed to play nice between the end of the first day and most of the second, he was now slowly drifting back to his old self. At least he wasn't telling Junsu to fuck off anymore. Now Kai was just constantly looking to him for entertainment.

"He even said the staff's services wouldn't be required since he had his bodyguards to take care of things," Zhang, the once unfortunate butler, had told him as they passed in the halls the night before. Junsu wasn't a butler or a maid, hell, he wasn't even really a bodyguard, but none of that stopped Kai from treating him like his very own personal thrall.

Still, Junsu wasn't about to complain. If he was honest with himself, he sort of liked the attention his future Omega was giving him.

"Good morning, Kaito. What are the plans for today?" he asked. They'd spent one full day together now with Junsu silently shadowing Kai. The young man wasn't too adventurous aboard the ship. After a pretty relaxing day, he'd asked where the ship's cinema was. Junsu had led the way and they'd ended up watching a movie together until it was time to turn in for the night.

It was one of the same movies that had been playing on the way over and Junsu had already seen it twice. Still, he sat through it for the third time, his eyes on Kai rather than the screen. He loved the way Kai giggled through all the best bits as if he were the only person in the room. Junsu had to admit, Kai was utterly adorable, tittering to himself in the dark of the cinema.

With a sigh, Junsu supposed all this running around would inevitably be a way to ingratiate himself with Kai. At the end of the week, he could reveal his true identity and it would be a big surprise but they'd both laugh it off in the end. Kai would realize that Junsu had proved himself to be a good Alpha who'd willingly wait on him hand and foot if necessary.

Junsu could do that. How hard could it be?

"Well," Kai started, responding to his earlier question and snapping Junsu out of his thoughts. "I'm going to start with breakfast."

Kai had gotten better at coming out of his room to eat, Junsu noted with a soft hum. Kai's eating habits were another one of his strange little quirks. He'd obviously been avoiding eating in front of people. Junsu wanted to ask about it but knew he couldn't. They didn't have that kind of relationship. He was just a bodyguard after all.

Kai hopped onto one of the tall stools across from Junsu and snapped at the waiter so that he could order something. The young woman came by, casting a wary glance Junsu's way as if to ask *are you sure about this?*

All the staff and most of the crew aboard the Zen Cruise Liner knew the little game Junsu was playing after Zhang spread the news like wildfire. Junsu simply tapped his lips before gazing thoughtfully over to Kai who was now perusing the short menu.

"Oh! Strawberry pancakes! I'll have those!"

"Of course, Omega Yamaguchi." The server bowed her head before walking away.

"It's so weird that the staff have to memorize everyone's names," Kai whispered loudly.

Junsu only chuckled. He sipped his tea, offering Kai some from the white porcelain pot in front of them as soon as the server came back quickly with a second cup.

"I always thought of people from Luxor as being coffee drinkers."

Junsu raised a brow and cocked his head to one side, unsure of what to say in response. "That's such a strange stereotype to have."

Kai simply shrugged. He poured himself some tea from the pot and tapped his cup against Junsu's with a rare little smile.

"Cheers," Junsu murmured with an amused huff.

Breakfast came and went after Kai scarfed his pancakes down with a vengeance. He leaned back in his chair with a satisfied sigh once he'd finished. He licked his lips, but there was whipped cream still stuck at the corner of his mouth.

Junsu chuckled. "You've got—" He touched the side of his own face.

Kai mirrored him.

"Wrong side. Here." Junsu reached out and thumbed Kai's lip gently. He was about to wipe his hand on a napkin, but instead licked the dollop of cream off his thumb.

"Hm," he moaned idly at the sweetness. "Maybe I should order that tomorrow."

Kai was staring at him with wide eyes before looking away. A small amount of color tinted his cheeks.

Junsu hid a smirk behind his teacup, but he didn't have time to take a sip. He almost spilled it all over himself when Kai stood suddenly, shaking the tall table as he hopped from his chair.

"Where's the spa on this boat?" he demanded, all his attitude pushing the shy, blushing part of his personality that had barely surfaced back into its void.

Junsu set his teacup back down and pointed the way, saying, "Just down those stairs two floors and turn left. It's at the end of the hall."

Kai nodded and made to leave without a word.

Junsu watched him for a while before turning back to his tea. He was about to pick his cup back up when Kai's voice cut through the tranquil calm of the morning.

"Um, aren't you coming?"

Junsu looked over his shoulder to see Kai standing at the stairs, staring at him with an impatient expression and a hand on his hip.

He almost laughed to himself out of shock. What the hell was he going to do with Kai at the spa? Were they going to get facials together? A couples massage? That would be entirely inappropriate considering they weren't actually a couple in this little game Junsu was playing.

Shaking his head, Junsu had no choice but to acquiesce to Kai's request.

"As you wish, Omega Yamaguchi," Junsu drawled as he stood from his chair and bowed.

His absurd formality had Kai glaring at him which in turn made Junsu stifle an amused huff of laughter. As entertaining as the situation was, he couldn't help but be hesitant in his movements. He followed Kai to the spa, wondering just how much further he could take this prank.

*

A liquid glaze of pure white greeted them when they entered the spa. The ambient sound of water dripping filled the entire room as simulated rain poured from the ceiling and landed squarely in pools between the walkways that led from the entrance to the reception desk. Branching in natural looking patterns, these walkways continued from there, leading to the different areas of the spa and bathhouses. On the roof, floodlights shone through massive tanks where koi fish swam about. They passed aimlessly through the overhead lighting while the shadows they cast moved fluidly below, floating through circular pools of light dotting the floor. A sweet scent filled the warm, humid air adding to the atmosphere, immediately relaxing all those who entered.

"Welcome, Omega Yamaguchi," a young Omega woman on staff at the front desk said in greeting as they arrived. "I do believe this is your first time with us. Have you perused our offerings already or would you like me to go over the many features this spa has to offer?"

"It's fine, I already know what I want. I'm booking the private baths for an hour." Kai slapped Junsu in the chest gently with the back of his hand and turned to smile at him. "I really miss the hot spring back home. The shower in my room on this boat is the worst and the bath is too small."

Junsu hummed, making a mental note of the complaint. If his future Omega enjoyed a nice bath, he'd have to look into getting a better one installed back at the house. A bigger one. Maybe they could slip in together and...

"Oh." The woman at the front desk let her eyes glide over to Junsu, cutting into his wandering thoughts. There was a subtle shift to the ever-present smile on her face, a twitching nerve at one corner of her lips. She turned back to Kai without faltering.

"Of course, Omega Yamaguchi. The Bamboo Bath is currently available. Will you be needing robes and towels for two?"

"Yes," Kai answered while Junsu simultaneously replied, "No."

Again, Kai slapped his chest. He smiled and waved Junsu's answer away as if he could make it disperse into the air like diffusing incense. "Yes. For two."

Junsu was in shock, but not so shocked that he didn't catch the smirk now sliding unhidden onto the receptionist's face. His eyes narrowed and her smile only grew wider. He made another mental note to add her to his list of traitors.

Moments later, a second attendant appeared carrying two robes and towels. She smiled at them and led the way to the baths. Kai and Junsu followed her through a transparent door and into the elaborate hall leading past the massage rooms. Other guests and staff moved beyond the wall, obscured from view behind the water flowing down along patterns in the frosted glass.

"Please make yourselves comfortable," the new attendant said as she opened the door and led them into an elegant room with a warmed wooden floor. Across the heated wooden boards was a square tub sunk into the center of the room, curtained on one side by a flowing shower of water and on the other two sides by lines of lush bamboo.

Kai gasped and Junsu blinked back his awe. He'd been to another part of the spa on the way over. That room had been nice, in a minimalist blindingly white sort of way. This indoor bamboo forest was astonishing. The lush green gave a beautiful impression of a natural scene. Beyond the bath, everything was polished wood all carved and latticed into traditional patterns commonly seen through the better-preserved parts of the Second Continent.

"I can't believe this is on a ship!" Kai clasped his hands together with a single excited clap, clearly keen to get into the water.

"The sauna and showers are through this way," their attendant told them. "If you're in need of anything at all, please simply ring this bell and I will return with haste."

Junsu nodded and said the thanks their attendant wasn't going to get out of Kai. The woman left him with a knowing smile that made him growl quietly deep in his chest. He was getting really sick of knowing smiles.

Changing and washing stations were located next to the tub with little cloth baskets, buckets, and dippers that seemed to be more for decoration than actual use. That was Junsu's impression at least. Whoever had designed the spa had created a perfect replica of a traditional Second Continent bathhouse and Kai seemed to be in his element.

Kai went over to one of the changing stations and started to undress, first dropping his shorts before moving to unlace the tie on the shirt that was still just barely preserving his modesty.

Junsu cleared his throat loudly. The fact Kai still didn't know he was his Alpha and yet he was behaving like this was making him uncomfortable, but he quickly realized that was Kai's exact intent.

"I shouldn't—" Junsu coughed to clear his throat again. "I should go."

Kai looked over one shoulder, shooting him a frown. "Stay."

"I don't think—"

Junsu's words died in his throat. Kai had untied his top and was starting to slip it off his shoulders ever so deliberately, revealing his gorgeous body. God, not only was he perfect, but his skin was a work of art, covered from neck to knee with a floral arrangement of traditional tattoos. The ink ended at his wrists, but Junsu could just make out the pink petals dancing along the joints of Kai's long, delicate fingers.

Junsu had seen many with these tattoos before when doing business with the leaders of the Second Continent. Kai's older brothers all bore them proudly, but theirs were dark: patterned in black and red and other warm colors. Junsu had never seen tattoos so pretty in every shade of pink and violet imaginable.

He sucked in a breath when Kai turned to him, his entire body on display. The one strip of his form that was free of tattoos practically begged Junsu's gaze to follow it down to the space between Kai's bare legs which offered a perfectly delicious view of his toned belly and flaccid length.

Kai's giggling laugh made him tear his eyes away and he stared over at the waterfall.

"It's perfectly natural," Kai teased. He clearly wasn't at all embarrassed by his own nudity.

"I really should go," Junsu protested.

"No, stay," Kai said again, stopping Junsu before he could head out of the door. "You're supposed to come with me everywhere, aren't you? Isn't that what my future Alpha is paying you for?"

Junsu gritted his teeth. He was used to being able to formulate coolly crafted retorts, but words were failing him as his brain function slowed in response to the open display of Kai's beauty.

"You can join me if you want," Kai said with a sly smile.

Junsu let out a heavy exhale. His future Omega was a little minx.

Finally relenting, Junsu went over to the dressing station and started to strip almost angrily. He pulled at his buttons so hard he was surprised none of them split off and scattered away.

Kai eyed him as he stripped, biting his lip. For an inappropriately long while, his teasing gaze travelled up and down Junsu's body and then he turned away and started to shower himself down.

Junsu turned as well, waiting until he heard the shower shut off. Soon after, Kai dipped into the tub with a soft sound like a single raindrop hitting the water.

Junsu finished taking off his pants and showered himself off quickly. As he cast a glance over one shoulder, he could see Kai leaning against the far edge of the pool, head back and eyes closed as he melted into the hot bath. The water was cloudy with minerals, thankfully, for the sake of Junsu's libido, obscuring Kai's stunning body.

Junsu politely used one of the available small modesty towels to cover the half-hard length of his cock as he walked over to the bath.

Kai opened his eyes and huffed out a little laugh as Junsu managed to slide into the water without revealing himself.

"People don't really do public baths in Luxor City, do they?" He wondered aloud, tilting his head to one side.

"We have bathhouses, so some people do. Older people, I guess," Junsu muttered as he sank deeper into the tub across from Kai. He closed his eyes and sighed as the warmth washed over him. He had to admit, it was an amazingly good bath.

"I think it's funny," Kai commented.

Junsu opened his eyes. He couldn't help but arch a brow at the little smirk twisting Kai's blushing red lips.

"What's funny?"

Kai shrugged, playing coy. "Just thinking out loud. It's funny to think you people in Luxor probably never see other people naked unless you're watching porn."

"Or having sex," Junsu replied without a beat. He smothered a laugh as Kai cutely sunk into the water up to the bottom of his nose and glared at him like an angry little alligator.

"You shouldn't tease me," he said when he resurfaced. A line of red cut his face in half, flushed from the water. This time Junsu really had to hold back that laugh.

"Why shouldn't I tease?" he asked, with a hand over his lips making it look like he was scratching his jaw as he hid a grin.

Kai pursed his lips and leaned forward. He moved in close, pressing against Junsu's arm. The perky point of a nipple rubbed against his bicep as if searching for friction.

Junsu was glad for the milky waters of the spa's mineral-rich bath because his cock was obscenely hard.

"Your boss wouldn't like you teasing his future Omega."

Junsu snorted, so close to being unable to contain himself, until he remembered who his boss was supposed to be. He didn't want to ruin his own reputation by being someone who his underlings laughed at. And so, serious as the grave, he replied, "He would not. No."

Kai smiled. He sunk back into the water and swam forward. When he fully resurfaced, it was with a seductive pout not two feet away.

"What would Junsu Sun do to you if he knew you were here with me?" Kai asked, one cheek dimpling as he smirked. "Like this?" he added, splashing a little bathwater onto Junsu's chest.

It was hard to answer, because he, Junsu, was not at all mad about enjoying a luxury spa with his future mate. He wanted to say "Junsu Sun would say he's enjoying himself" but considering his current disguise he had to think of it differently. He thought of the real Jaemin and what he would do if he found out the man had been flirting with his future Omega in this same situation.

He furrowed his brow.

"Junsu Sun would probably have me take a very long walk off a very short pier in a very heavy pair of concrete shoes."

Kai stared at him wide-eyed. Then, after a stunned silence, he let out a little burst of laughter.

"I'm sorry." He covered his mouth to hide a smile. "Oh my god, I shouldn't laugh. He's probably going to kill you."

Junsu shrugged. "I can handle it," he quipped right back.

A warmth not caused by the steaming bathwater spread through his chest, as he prided himself on making Kai laugh again. His future Omega leaned in and patted his cheek, smacking it with his dripping hand.

"Don't worry," Kai said with a titter in his tone. "This will be our little secret."

The real Jaemin might have found those words comforting, but Junsu didn't. He pursed his lips into a flat line and closed his eyes once more, leaning back in the water. He wasn't sure about any of this anymore. The game had gone too far.

He was in too deep.

*

They sat together in one of the private saunas attached to the bamboo room to dry off after the bath. There were two, one smelling of smoke and smoldering earth and a second smelling of cloves and cinnamon. Safe to say, Kai preferred the lush, sweet scent of the second.

Thankfully for the sake of Junsu's sanity, Kai had covered himself with a towel. As tiny as the thing was, it proved a godsend. Junsu had never considered himself a prude, far from it, but he definitely wasn't used to seeing anyone naked outside a strip club or the bedroom. Especially not in such an intimate setting. It wasn't completely unheard of for an unmated Alpha and Omega pair to enjoy time together like they were, but it definitely wasn't what most would call common either.

Kai was fresh and clean from the bath, but his luscious Omega scent was quickly resurfacing. Junsu resisted the urge to breathe it in deep. Kai's scent blossomed floral with a touch of sea salt. Thankfully, he was clearly taking suppressants, a medication designed to stop Omegas from slipping into a seasonal heat and somewhat dull their pheromonal scent. Despite that fact, Junsu was still affected. His keen Alpha senses could pick out Kai's suppressed scent. Maybe it spoke to how truly compatible they were? He wouldn't know unless he asked Kai if he felt it too. And that wasn't gonna happen, not until this little ruse came to an end at least.

"What should we do next?" Kai asked, pulling Junsu out of his reverie. His voice was breathy and relaxed, his entire body visibly lax from the warmth.

"What do you want to do?" Junsu asked.

Kai let out an annoyed little sigh. "It's not fair if I have to come up with everything. I'm trying to entertain us both here. So..." He side-eyed Junsu and repeated, "What do *you* want to do?"

"Well, there's a bar in the lower decks," Junsu suggested. "You can drink better stuff then they've got on the upper decks and people gamble with real money instead of those little chips you get in the casino." He smirked at the scandalized awe filling Kai's eyes. "I could show you down there? Most of the guests don't know about it."

"Ooh, sounds exclusive! Let's go!" Kai jumped up, forgetting about his towel. It fell to the ground and he leaned over to pick it up with a huff of, "oops."

Junsu knew he shouldn't have looked, but it was too late. He stared along the length of Kai's bending form, tracing the curve of his body until...their eyes met.

A dark gaze peered up from beneath long lashes. Kai stayed as he was a moment longer than was necessary. Then, with a smirk, he straightened and left without a word.

Junsu watched the heavy wood door close and all he could do was sit and think: *My god, what is happening?*

He followed Kai out and avoided his gaze as they both showered off and dressed. Out of the corner of his eye, Kai's body turned toward him almost as if he was trying to get Junsu's attention without words. The movement was probably unconscious, Junsu surmised. He was an Alpha and Kai was an Omega, they were clearly compatible, and their bodies reached out to each other somewhat unwittingly. Junsu tried to keep his eyes from shifting over in Kai's direction as he buttoned his shirt.

"Should we eat first?"

That question came from a lot closer than he'd been expecting. Junsu almost jumped as he looked to his left and saw Kai not one inch from his face, chin practically resting on his shoulder.

"Uh," Junsu muttered. "Probably?"

Kai smiled and moved past him with a nod. "Okay!"

Junsu finished buttoning his shirt and followed after him. Kai was in a startlingly good mood. Junsu made a mental note to tip the spa staff on his way out of the door.

"How was it?" the woman at the front desk asked as they exited the flowing hall and came back into the reception area.

Kai hummed delightedly but didn't answer. He simply continued through the room and out into the hall.

"It was perfect. Thank you so much," Junsu said, sliding her a crisp bill.

The woman hummed as Kai had done and plucked it up. With a smirk, she tucked it into her bra. "So, Alpha Sun, when are you going to tell him?" she asked, slipping immediately into a more casual tone despite her use of his formal title.

Junsu's only response was a soft groan. Without answering, he turned to leave, though he could hear her calling after him, "The spa staff have a pool going against the housekeepers! One thousand says before the bonding!"

Pausing, Junsu frowned for the split second it took him to realize what she was talking about. *Mating before the bonding? Ha!*

"Not going to happen," Junsu chuckled. Thank god Kai was already gone. He didn't know about Kai's family, but his mother would kill him if he broke that tradition.

*

Junsu stepped out of the spa and directly into Kai.

"What were you two talking about?" Kai asked as soon as Junsu popped out through the doors. He'd been waiting in the hall and his hands were now in fists pressed to his hips.

"We were—" Junsu blinked rapidly, searching for an answer. "I was just asking if we can get food at the bar lower down. Turns out we can so no need to walk all the way over to the dining room to grab something to eat."

"Great! Lead the way," Kai said with a gesture. He waved Junsu ahead of him and followed him once more through the ship's winding halls.

They went down two more floors until they were deep in the body of the boat. There were no windows in these corridors and the lights were dimmed to match the mood of the atmospheric music playing. It was slow with a deep bass Kai couldn't help but sway to as he walked.

Junsu followed behind him. His gaze traced Kai's every move, following the sway of his hips. They made their way through a small but thoroughly occupied card club that drew Kai's attention. He paused to watch a game for a moment before he skipped along to catch up with Junsu.

The bar was right next to the card club and it wasn't nearly so busy. They sat down at a table draped with a red cloth and were immediately handed menus by an overly attentive waiter.

Over the top of his menu, Junsu looked across at Kai. His face glowed healthily from the spa. The red-shaded lamp between them lit his features in a way that would have been darkly ominous, but Kai's cheeks were so smooth the shadows softened and left him looking warm and sanguine.

Junsu sucked in a breath and went back to perusing his menu. He was still nervous about the current situation, his impersonation, the bonding, but in spite of everything, he was really growing to like Kai. The past two days had been quite nice, and they only had four more. Maybe now would be a good time to end the charade, to reveal himself, they were both so relaxed and settled in to eat. What could go wrong?

Junsu lowered his menu and took a deep breath.

"Kai."

"Mm-hm?" Kai looked up from his menu, his soft eyes landing on Junsu.

Junsu let out the breath he was holding and sat up straight. He was about to open his mouth to speak when their server came by.

"Good afternoon! Let me get you started with the soup of the day," he said, setting sloshing bowls down in front of them.

Kai hummed and was already lifting his spoon to eat, despite the server waiting to take his main order. He waved at Junsu, gesturing for him to go first.

"Ah," Junsu breathed. He had never been so flustered in his life. Shaking his head, he ordered the crab cakes while Kai ordered some fried marinated tuna.

"And to drink?"

"Let's do a bottle of rice wine!" Kai said excitedly. "When I was little, I always used to drink milk after a bath, but we can be naughty now."

Junsu almost choked on a breath. How did Kai manage to go from being a little minx in the spa to this wonderfully cheery cute thing telling him about his childhood?

The waiter looked to Junsu for confirmation, and he nodded. "Yes, a bottle and two cups."

"I'll be right back with your orders." The waiter took their menus and walked off.

"This is really different from upstairs," Kai said as soon as the waiter was gone. His gaze travelled around the bar. "It's not as classy or bright, but I kind of like it. It gives you a mysterious feeling, doesn't it? Like something out of a spy movie."

Distracted now from his confession, Junsu chuckled and looked around. The bar was indeed a moodier, more mellowed out version of the shining bright dining hall up above. There was an element of mystery surrounding the dim, crimson-lit room, an element of romance. When Junsu's eyes returned to Kai, he could see the Omega staring off down the hall. Seeming to notice Junsu's gaze, he turned back with an excited expression.

"Do you play cards?" Kai asked.

The question seemed to have come out of nowhere, but looking down the hall, Junsu realized there were slatted openings and archways in the far wall leading out into the card club floor. Kai was intent on the play happening between two Alphas nearby and the bets being placed on their game.

"No, I prefer Mah-jongg or dice," Junsu replied with a huff of a laugh.

"Mah-jongg? Are you like secretly eighty years old?" Kai snorted, shaking his head and muttering "Mah-jongg" to himself. "I'll show you a real game later."

Junsu smiled and did the same. "And maybe I'll show you Mah-jongg."

Kai stuck out his tongue and turned away, again looking out across the room. He was clearly still trying to make out what was going on in the game being played that he had some interest in. He peered over, avidly watching the game and allowing Junsu to watch him.

Their food came, followed quickly by their wine in a fine porcelain flask. They tapped their cups together and drank.

They talked about small things. Kai gushed about his life back in the Second Continent, comparing the spa they'd just enjoyed to his family's private hot springs back home and other spa resorts he'd been to.

Junsu listened to him with a small smile tilting his lips. Nothing, it seemed, could ever be good enough for this Omega. He'd usually be annoyed by that sort of personality, but Kai was weirdly starting to grow on him. Maybe because he wasn't used to having someone treat him with such a dismissive attitude. He kind of liked it. Kai was going to be a challenge to please, and Junsu liked a challenge.

Despite there only being about ten people in the bar, a singer appeared on a small stage. She serenaded them with a lighter sort of music than what had been playing for ambience before. Kai watched her with a softening expression while Junsu didn't for a moment take his eyes off Kai. After the first song finished people clapped, but Kai merely turned back to him with an unchanged expression.

"Tell me more about Junsu Sun."

The man himself sucked in a breath and leaned back in his chair. He frowned. What was that tightness in his chest? Was he actually feeling jealous of himself?

"I don't know, last time you weren't happy with what I told you," Junsu muttered.

Kai bit his lip, wetting it as he looked up thoughtfully. "Okay. But you're his friend or something, right?"

"We're...very close."

"Yeah, so tell me about him. I just want to know what he's like."

Junsu sighed. "Well, Junsu also plays Mah-jongg."

There was silence. Then Kai burst out laughing. "Okay, so you two sit around like old men and play Mah-jongg. I get it. What else?"

Junsu shifted in his seat and reached out to down his drink. "You know the photo you sent him?"

Kai scoffed. "Ugh, that stupid photo. Yeah. What about it?"

"It's very beautiful."

Kai looked across at him, his wide eyes glowing with curiosity.

"Junsu thinks it's very beautiful," he said, correcting himself. He cleared his throat and leaned back. "He told me you looked lovely in that robe and how you were lit like an angel in that garden. He said you looked stunning, but..."

"But?" Kai cut in. His brow furrowed and his tone gave Junsu pause. Again, he sounded so vulnerable.

"I know he's going to like the real you a lot more." Junsu smiled softly. "You're just so amazingly unique."

The lamplight disguised it well, but Junsu knew the young Omega across from him was blushing.

Kai looked away, shy suddenly.

"Did—did you see it too?"

"Yes," Junsu replied without hesitation. "And I agreed with him completely."

"Oh." Kai sucked in a breath. He seemed a little shaken. Junsu could practically hear his heart pounding in his chest.

"I—I want to go back to my room now," he said, standing suddenly. "Please."

With a concerned arch to his brow, Junsu stood as well. He waved to the waiter, signaling their intent to depart, before leading Kai out of the lounge. He pressed a gentle hand to Kai's lower back as they walked through the halls.

"Are you feeling okay?" he asked once they got up the stairs and outside into the fresh air for a moment.

Kai nodded, but he didn't speak the entire walk back to his room.

When they reached his door, he did not enter right away. They stood outside in the empty hall, both seeming unsure of what to say to the other, but neither of them ready to part ways just yet. So, they just stood there, almost toe to toe, staring at each other.

"I know I might have...acted odd," Kai started slowly.

"I'm just still hoping you had a nice time," Junsu replied.

"I did. It was nice. But I just sort of realized something." Kai frowned. "I don't—I don't want to talk about Junsu anymore."

The man in question sucked in a breath, though he tried not to look too insulted. Kai wasn't talking about him. Not really.

"Why not?" Junsu asked, deadpan as possible, trying to keep any and all emotion out of his voice.

"I don't really know Junsu yet," Kai whispered. "And it feels weird hearing about him before I actually get to know him. I don't—I don't know. I just—I'm here with you now so I..."

As Kai trailed off and looked down at his soft canvas shoes, Junsu was left trying to read him with a perplexed uncertainty.

"Kai? What are you trying to say?"

Junsu could see something inside Kai was tearing him apart, as if he was trying to figure something out in his mind, something that left him completely disoriented.

Kai's eyes eventually rose once more. His cautious gaze met Junsu's.

"I don't know," he whispered again.

Both confused and unsure, they stood there together. Kai sucked in a breath. He was clearly overwhelmed with an inexplicable sensation. Junsu knew that feeling; he could feel it, too, though the haze he was in was the culmination of irrational jealousy and guilt and... complete adoration for the Omega standing before him.

"Hey! Jaemin!"

Junsu heard the call, but he was so busy staring down at Kai, he didn't answer right away.

"Jae? *Jaemin*?" The voice called again, this time enunciating the name expectantly.

Only when a little frown creased Kai's brow did Junsu realize the mood was gone. He was well beyond the point where he should have answered. It looked odd.

"Yeah!" he called back. Finally unlocking himself from Kai's gaze, he cast a glance over his shoulder and saw the real Jaemin and Shik standing at the other end of the deck. They glared expectantly at him, both wearing serious expressions that Junsu hadn't seen since before their vacation started.

They were here for business.

"We need to talk," the real Jaemin said.

Shik was at his side, nodding. "Empire matters," they added.

Junsu momentarily looked back to Kai whose expression had done a complete one-eighty.

He seemed less than unimpressed, glaring at the other two bodyguards down the hall.

"Duty calls," he said with a click of his tongue. His eyes rolled and he turned away and opened the door to his room. It slammed shut behind him before Junsu could speak.

"Guys..." Junsu all but growled. He stormed over to his friends who had their hands raised in yielding poses.

"This isn't a joke or anything," Jaemin said. "Xijuan called."

"She received information that we may have an issue on board," Shik clarified. They looked around at the doors. "We should talk somewhere more secure. Let's go."

Calming, Junsu nodded and led the other two to his suite.

Seven: In Too Deep

As they moved away from Kai's room, neither Jaemin nor Shik mentioned the scene in the hall. They waited for Junsu to pass before following him silently. Once they arrived in Junsu's room, Shik laid out a data screen and all three of them crowded around the small dining table by the window.

"So, you remember the Underground group we took out before the cruise," Shik started, as their fingers worked over the keyboard. A familiar document came up on screen. The data hovered in the air between them. Lines of light summarized detailed three-dimensional profiles, photos, and other miscellaneous information about the Underground organization. "You know? The ones who were running the brothel by the west docks? Importing Omegas from the Second Continent?"

Jaemin gestured as Shik spoke, noting the photos that had been highlighted red and marked with the word *neutralized.*

"It was just over a week ago. Of course, I remember," Junsu snapped. "Look, I was having a nice evening before you two interrupted so just get to the point."

Jaemin and Shik seemed surprised by his sour mood, but they didn't say anything.

Ignoring Junsu's attitude, Shik simply went on, "Now that the Southern Empire's intelligence organizations have started merging with the Second Continent's, we received intel from the Yamaguchi family that someone who boarded this ship might be involved with the trafficking."

Junsu's eyes narrowed. "Were they using this ship?" he hissed, disgusted. "Of course, it makes sense." Ever since the Sun Family had found out that Jimena Faraji had escaped his exile from Luxor City by stowing away on one of their cargo ships, those boats were checked and rechecked for contraband at every port of entry. However, the same sort of regulations had not been applied to private cruise lines like the one they were currently sailing on.

Jaemin crossed his arms over his chest and nodded to the document. "Whoever they are, they're coming over to Luxor to take over where Naoto Kim left off. To restart the business as it were. Your mother wants us to make sure we find them and nab them on board before they get a chance to disappear into the city."

Junsu hummed. It was a good plan. Luxor was a big place and now with the borders opening up, they'd probably lose these Underground gangsters as soon as they landed.

"Who are we talking about here? Some underling? Or is this someone who's going to have some real pull?"

Jaemin gritted his teeth before answering. "As far as I've heard, this main guy was their collector. He's an Alpha, the one who found the Omegas for Naoto and sent them over. That's why he was still over in the Second

Continent and why the Yamaguchi family had a watch on any of his supposed movements."

Shik nodded. "Kazue Yamaguchi is keen to see justice done. When we catch him, the Yamaguchi family want him dead, but they said we can interrogate him as much as we'd like beforehand to find out who else in this gang is still hanging around on our turf."

"Good," Junsu replied. He could feel himself slipping back into his old skin again. He sat straight and tense, cool and calm. He wasn't some lovesick Alpha; he was the heir to the Southern Empire of Luxor City. This was just what he needed to remember that.

Junsu stood from his seat and paced in front of the glass window overlooking the rolling ocean, black under the evening sky. He stared out over the patio to the pale line of the moonlit horizon.

"Does the intel give us anywhere to start?" he asked.

"Unfortunately, they don't know what he looks like, boss," Shik said. "He goes by Nam, but who knows if he'll be using an alias."

"The Second Continent has been aware of him for a long time, but he's a fucking ghost," Jaemin added.

"If he's not an idiot, he'd better fucking ghost," Junsu muttered. "Be on the lookout."

"Oh, boss, one more thing," Jaemin cut in before they could be dismissed. "Xijuan was particular in adding that, knowing Kaito is on board, the Yamaguchi family are very concerned about this whole business. They don't want to bother him with it because he's supposed to be on a holiday, but they want your assurance that no harm will come to him."

"They have it," Junsu replied without hesitation. "We'll have this dealt with as quietly as possible and I won't let Kaito out of my sight."

*

Unfortunately for Junsu, it wasn't up to him if Kai wanted to be in or out of his sight.

The next day, Kai had ordered someone from the cruise line to ring Junsu on the phone in his room. The shrill tone woke him up far earlier than he would have liked.

"Hello?"

"I know this isn't actually Jaemin Yi, but I had a request to call him from Kaito Yamaguchi and assumed it was you he meant for me to call, Alpha Sun," the amused sounding receptionist said in a cheery tone.

Junsu groaned. "Probably. Okay what is it?"

"Omega Yamaguchi left a message for you. He has asked us to have breakfast sent up to his room and requested that no one bother him until dinner."

"Including me?"

"Including—well—especially you, Alpha Sun. Thus, the phone call."

Junsu accepted this with a grunt. He thanked the receptionist and hung up the phone. With a soft sigh, he fell back against his pillows and stared up at the ceiling. Kaito clearly wasn't happy with how they'd left things the night before, though Junsu wasn't sure what had happened. The entire day's events were a blur in his sleep-addled brain. This painful mix of business and pleasure was a terrible thing.

Junsu rolled out of bed and decided to use the time he'd now been graciously given to investigate the information he'd received the night before from Jaemin and Shik. He walked the entire length of the ship, searching for suspicious characters and familiar faces.

During his infiltration of the Underground, he'd met many shady nameless men whose positions in the gang remained a mystery to him. Junsu hoped to find one of these familiar faces onboard, but nothing turned up. There wasn't much he could do without getting the staff involved. He would try something else later.

The day passed swiftly and that evening around dinner, Junsu went to Kai's room. Junsu knocked once and then a few more times. There was no answer and no shuffling beyond the door. Kaito was either a really deep sleeper or he wasn't in there.

Standing outside, puzzled, Junsu looked around warily. Undecided about what to do next, he paced in front of the door until he saw the butler, Zhang, come around the hall with a pile of fresh linens in hand.

"Hey, Jun—I mean—Jaemin!" Zhang said with an innocuous wink. "What are you up to today?"

"Nothing interesting. Do you know where Kai went?" Junsu asked, gesturing with a thumb to the Omega's bedroom door.

"Oh, I think he left after lunch or sometime around then," Zhang answered with a shrug. He went to the door and unlocked it with a master key. "I remember him saying something about planning to get a massage or a facial or something down in the spa. I'm not sure though. I came by and asked if he wanted fresh towels. He seemed pissed, stomping around and muttering to himself. Don't wanna assume anything, but I think it was about you. What did you guys get up to yesterday that ticked him off like that? I thought things were calming down."

Junsu didn't answer. He simply gave Zhang a pat on the back and went on his way, leaving the man calling after him. "Ju—Jae! I was just kidding!" Nearly dropping his linens, Zhang almost said the wrong name again.

Junsu waved at him over one shoulder without turning back. He strode out of sight, determined to find Kai.

The ship was grand and luxurious, but it wasn't that big once you knew your way around. Still, somehow there were too many places to look for one person, especially in the evening. Junsu started in the dining hall but when his search there came up empty, he continued around to places they'd been before. He passed by the spa and asked the receptionist if she'd seen Kai, but again, his enquiry turned up nothing except for the information that he'd been in for a facial a few hours back, sometime after lunch, like Zhang had already told him.

Junsu moved on to the outer decks, the sunroof, and then the cinema before finally heading down to the lower decks. He walked through the crowded card club and up to the bar. It was quiet as it had been the night before and there was no sign of Kai.

With a soft huff of frustration, Junsu shook his head and walked back down the hall. What was he supposed to do? Wait all night outside the Omega's door? He was sure he'd get shooed away as soon as Kai returned from whatever secret little spot he was currently enjoying.

Junsu huffed. He was about to give up and just go enjoy a drink with Jaemin and Shik when a familiar laugh caught his attention.

Determined, he stepped through the red arches that led back into the card club and was immediately greeted by a concierge. Junsu waved the man away; he was only there for one reason and said reason was sitting at a table, grinning broadly as he slammed down a card with a loud slap.

"The brights and the rain man!" Kai gave a victorious cheer. "That's this round done!"

Junsu approached the table at a deliberate pace that heavily contrasted his previously rushed searching around the ship. Kai was clearly at the end of a game as he'd just put down what Junsu could only assume was a winning set. The Alphas surrounding Kai groaned as their money was slowly taken from the pool at the center of the table and added to the grinning young Omega's growing pile.

"Kai," Junsu drawled in curt greeting, trying to keep the annoyance out of his tone. He didn't want to let the Omega know how long he'd been searching for him.

"Oh, *you're* here! Everyone, this is the bodyguard I was telling you about," Kai drawled. He had clearly been drinking, though not so much that he couldn't still kick ass at cards. "Some bodyguard he is, am I right? It's been hours! Any of you could have taken advantage of me seven times over by now!" Kai winked coquettishly.

There were only Alphas around the playing table, and they all laughed brutishly, enjoying Kai's crude humor. A rank musk hung in the air, competing with the subtle sweetness of Kai's suppressant-muted scent. Junsu could tell by smell alone that each and every one of the Alphas present was vying to lure Kai back to their rooms for the night.

Junsu growled low and deep in his chest. "How much have you had to drink?" he whispered as he came to stand behind Kai's plush chair.

Not answering at first, Kai simply lifted a glass to his lips and sipped the cocktail within. He set it down and shrugged.

"Enough," he eventually replied before adding, "or rather, not nearly enough!"

Junsu gritted his teeth as another round of laughter made its way around the table, but he didn't protest. He knew better than to try to get Kai to leave with him. He'd proved to be an arrogant little thing and would probably throw a fit if push came to shove. Especially after he'd had a few.

Junsu was sure any attempt to hustle Kai back to his room would prompt one of the idiot Alphas to defend him and no doubt they'd soon have a fight on their hands. It was a better tactic to simply stay and wait it out. Like an overexcited child, Kai would get bored with his cards and tire himself out eventually.

And so Junsu waited. He stood over the group, watching as the dealer laid out the cards. It looked like he was decorating the table with a series of pictures: maple leaves, hills, ribbons, peonies...There was a vast assortment of designs that weren't clearly connected in Junsu's regard. Eight cards were placed face up in the center of the table while a hand was passed face down to each of the players with their elaborate pictures hidden from view.

Kai picked up his hand and Junsu observed the sets of images over his shoulder with a deep frown.

"How do you even play with cards like that?" Junsu asked. He'd never seen the game before.

Kai looked back over one shoulder. If Junsu read his expression correctly, Kai thought he was joking. "They're flower cards obviously. They're pretty common in the Second Continent and— Oh!" Kai plucked a card out of his hand and showed them to the table. "I see a full month of matching suits! Redeal!"

Again, the Alphas around the table groaned and muttered. It seemed to be some arbitrary rule, but Kai had won that round automatically and the game was reset for the next. Most of them had bet against Kai. How were they supposed to know he'd win his second game in a row? Some shook their heads and seemed mildly amused while others were frowning. The Alpha who Kai was playing against was practically foaming at the mouth.

The dealer took Kai's cards and gave him a new hand.

Junsu was left utterly confused. Kai had won with a set of four different cards before the dealer took them away and, for the life of him, he couldn't tell how they were matching.

"Some kind of circle, some birds and little hills. I don't understand, those don't go together at all." As he voiced his confusion, it earned him a round of haughty laughter.

Kai reached back and patted Junsu's hand. "You're so cute, Alpha Johnny-come-lately. It was a matching suit. I had all of August. The grass cards."

Junsu shook his head. "They all happened to have a little hill somewhere in the background, so they were the same?"

"It isn't called a *little hill*. It's grass. But yes," Kai replied almost passively, focused on the new cards in his hand and those laid out on the table before him.

"But—" Junsu started, still confused, "how were they matching?"

"They weren't matching, they were all different cards from the same grass set and grass is August, so they made a full set for the month. Because I got lucky and they were dealt right to me on my turn, I won the round and got points," Kai replied as if it were the most obvious thing in the world.

He looked to the others across the table and rolled his eyes. Some of them chuckled, shaking their heads at Junsu.

These Second Continent Alphas didn't know who he was; he could tell they all just thought he was some New American idiot who didn't know how their cards worked.

Still puzzled, Junsu went on, "But one had birds and the sun?"

"Again, not the sun, that was the moon."

"Still—"

"Ugh, you're such a Luxor City island boy. Look, it's the same as your dumb western cards," Kai huffed, gesturing to two of the flower cards in his hand. The purple wisteria flowers within the card's black frame fell in near identical patterns but one had a red ribbon in front of it. "The queen of hearts and the ace of hearts don't look the same, but they're a matching suit. Same with the grass, the other grass, the moon and the grass, the grass and the birds. They're the same suit."

With a hum, Junsu felt he was beginning to understand. He leaned over Kai's chair, gazing down at his cards and comparing them with those on the table.

Junsu observed a few turns. Kai and the Alpha he was playing against collected cards one at a time from the center of the table to create sets. Each round they were awarded points based on a variety of sets like the one Kai had just explained to him. The game seemed familiar, but it took a minute for Junsu to put two and two together.

"Is this game...Go Fish?"

Kai scoffed. "Don't be ridiculous. We wouldn't gamble on a game of Go Fish."

Junsu watched as one Alpha at the opposite end of the table made a match with two iris flower cards, gaining himself a blue ribbon.

"So, what's this game called?" he asked.

"It's called Koi-Koi."

"Koi..." Junsu drew out the word with a raised brow. "Like the fish? Like *Go Fish*?"

Kai tilted his head back, staring up at Junsu silently for a second before letting out a long-suffering sigh. He waved away the coincidence and turned his attention back to the game.

Junsu leaned over to watch the next play. It was nearly Kai's turn, and by the look on his face, the Omega had already calculated that he'd have another winning set in no time. They went around the table once and Kai made a few small matches. By the time they got to his second turn he was ready to set up his final hand. On the third turn he collected a card with a cup and set it next to another flower card he'd picked up before and declared victory.

"I've got a set with the cherry blossom bright and the sake! Points please!" Kai cheered with a wide smile.

He was clearly over the moon. How his luck had won him three hands in a row, Junsu didn't know, but he could tell that some of the Alphas sitting around the table with money on the game were not happy about it.

*

"This is fucking bullshit! At least call and let the round go on so someone else even has a chance to win!" the man across from Kai snapped. Shaking his head, he slammed his useless cards down on the table. He'd been fuming earlier and had never calmed down.

Kai snorted at the Alpha's overt display of emotion. He placed his old cards down lightly on the table and pushed them toward the dealer who quickly refreshed his hand and started a new round.

"Well," he said as he picked up his newly dealt hand, "someone's being a sore loser."

"How did you come to be so good at cards?" a much more civil Alpha asked him. She smiled at Kaito, clearly more than willing to part with her money if she got a chance to woo a cute little Omega like him.

Kai smiled and was about to tell them all about how his three older brothers now very much regretted teaching him all their tricks, but before he could, the disgusting Alpha at the far end of the table spat out a vile laugh.

"Little bitch is just good at hiding cards up that Omega cunt of his."

The air grew tense. A few of the other Alphas scoffed at the rudeness, tutting and shaking their heads. It was unheard of to say such vulgar words in front of an Omega, especially one whose tattoos clearly marked him as a revered member of a powerful family from the Second Continent.

"Relax, man. It's just a fucking game," one of his fellows muttered, gaze shifting between Kai and the seething Alpha.

Kai stared at the furious man, his lips parted in an expression of disbelief. He let out a single breathless laugh before looking down at the cards in his hand. Clearing his throat, he chose to ignore the Alpha in favor of the cards being laid out in front of them.

*

As the confrontation played out, Junsu bristled. He was holding himself back from lunging across the cards and knocking some much-needed sense into the asshole Alpha at the other end of the room. He gritted his teeth and for a moment it seemed as if everyone was just going to ignore this revolting Alpha's rudeness, but then a small smile split Kai's lips.

With his new cards in hand, Kai slowly placed one of his cards on the table. He picked up the moon card and was quickly dealt another that gave him a set with the sake cup again. Just like that, he collected another game-ending match right off the bat.

Drawing away, he raised a brow. Kai raised his chin up and stared down his nose at the rude Alpha across from him. He leaned closer to the man as he moved to pass his cards back to the dealer and refill his hand. As he did this, he murmured something Junsu didn't quite hear.

The words were in another language, one with which Junsu was vaguely familiar, mixed with something that had to be Second Continent slang, which went right over his head. However, the leering cheekiness in Kai's tone was crystal clear and it soon became very obvious that the Alpha, unlike Junsu, understood exactly what he was saying.

The next thing anyone knew, the furious Alpha was on his feet. He stood so fast that his chair tipped back. It slammed against the polished black floor. He reached forward with a blue-veined hand and angrily grabbed a fistful of the collar of Kai's shirt before pulling him out of his chair and halfway across the table.

"You're gonna regret that, you little—"

He didn't get the chance to complete his threat. Junsu was on him, one hand breaking the man's hold on Kai while the other balled into a fist and landed a blow that cut the disgruntled Alpha across the chin. At the awkward angle, it sent his head crashing down against the arm of his chair.

Everyone around the table got to their feet. Most of the Alphas collected their cash while others simply sprung up and fled. The rest of the room turned to watch with eager expressions as a member of staff dialed for security in the corner.

The vile Alpha picked himself up off the ground, holding his jaw with one hand. His eyes flared as they landed on Junsu and he growled low and deep.

There were two others with him all of a sudden. One had been at their table; the other came over from the nearby bar. While they hadn't been appreciative of how he'd talked about the Omega moments before, they were clearly on the rude Alpha's side in a fight.

Three against one were pretty bad odds, but Junsu had already half concussed the first asshole. He smirked. *What's two more?*

As one Alpha lunged at him, Junsu dodged the blow while putting a chair in the man's way. He then kicked the table into the already injured Alpha before picking up a deck of cards and throwing them in the third guy's face.

By that time, the man who'd lunged at Junsu had recovered. He twisted around and landed a punch just as Junsu was turning to confront him again. A ring on the man's fist caught Junsu right in the lip, drawing blood.

Covering his face, Junsu lashed out with a kick in response. He landed a heel in the man's chest and sent him crashing back into another table. The Alphas there all stood with angered shouts. They were just as pissed as Junsu at having their game interrupted and their rage pulled the man into a second fight.

One down.

The man who'd had cards thrown in his face was rounding on Junsu now. He went straight for him, which just meant he was giving momentum for his own downfall. Junsu grabbed his wrist as his fist skimmed past his face and twisted it until the man was forced to his knees. He then dealt the man a blow to the head that sent him groaning down onto the floor. He wouldn't be getting up anytime soon.

One to go.

The final Alpha, the instigator, was sneering from his place across the table. He eyed Junsu and then stumbled toward Kai who'd practically frozen as soon as the fight started. The man moved to grab him, but Junsu was across the room in no time flat. He cracked an elbow against the man's skull and sent him out like a light.

Junsu was panting; he could barely hear the murmuring from the crowd that had gathered to watch. A few of the other patrons were exchanging money to one happy-looking member of staff who'd clearly called a bet on the whole mess.

Junsu eyed the groaning incapacitated men before turning to Kai. He rushed to the Omega, wrapped an arm around him, and led him from the room just as the ship's onboard security came in to see what all the fuss was about.

"Are you all right?" Junsu whispered as they made their way down the hall, far from the fray. "That piece of shit. I can't believe anyone would talk to you like that. And how dare he lay a fucking hand on you."

Kai was silent most of the way back up out of the ship and to the deck. When they reached the outer decks, a grin spread wide across his face.

"What was that? You're amazing!" Kai cheered. "I was kind of in shock for a second. Damn! I wish I'd taken a bet out on you. Wow!"

Junsu let out a huffing laugh. He slipped his arm from around the Omega seeing as he was all right, but Kai sidled up close to him.

"Oh," he said. His brows arched as he moved in close, checking something on Junsu's face. "You're hurt."

"It's fine. Just a cracked lip." Junsu shook his head, batting away Kai's hand gently as he touched his face, thumb just running past the bloody split in the bottom swell of his lip. It really didn't hurt that bad. Still, Junsu winced.

"No seriously! You're hurt!" Kai exclaimed. "It's bleeding. I have some ointment for that sort of thing. Come with me to my room."

It wasn't a request; it was an order. Junsu let out a resigned sigh and allowed Kai to lead him to the suite.

He hadn't been inside Kai's room but, as he'd assumed, it was much like his own. They had been booked in two of the largest rooms aboard the ship, courtesy of Xijuan Sun. Junsu's mother had said she'd wanted them as comfortable as possible. Well, she probably hadn't been expecting this.

Junsu was sitting on a chair at the small table in Kai's suite massaging his reddened hands. He could already feel his knuckles starting to get sore and swell slightly. He'd probably have stiff fingers tomorrow. Maybe they could take another trip to the spa. Did they do hand massages?

Junsu's sporadic thoughts were sidetracked as Kai slammed down a small wooden case. The move forced Junsu to place a hand on the table. He managed to stop the glass surface from wobbling until it shattered.

"Here we go," Kai said as he opened the case. "I brought a lot of little things from home. I wasn't really sure if I'd be able to get them in Luxor."

Junsu watched as he pulled a small metal container with an intricately decorative label and glass bottle of liquid from the case with a small white flower on it. He handed that to Junsu and told him to put it on his hands while he opened the metal container and started dabbing his pinky into the substance therein.

Junsu looked at the familiar medicinal oil and chuckled.

"You can definitely get this in Luxor...in the Southern Empire, at least," he said with absolute certainty. It wasn't just the bottle; the strong smell filled his chest with a nostalgic sense of warmth. "I don't use the stuff myself, but my Omega mom used to swear by it. I remember going to the shops, picking it up from the apothecary for her when I was little."

Kai cocked his head to one side. "She used to?"

"Yeah," Junsu breathed, closing his eyes. "She... passed away."

"I'm sorry."

"It was a long time ago." Junsu set the bottle back down, smiling sadly. "Anyway, you can get this in Luxor. No need to worry."

Kai rolled his eyes and took Junsu's chin in his hand, drawing his eyes up from the bottle. "Well, I wouldn't have known that," he huffed. "Open."

Junsu parted his lips and allowed Kai's pinkie finger to dab the ointment over the cracked split in his skin that was still red but no longer bleeding. He somehow managed not to wince as the strong-smelling stuff sunk into his skin.

"People keep telling me the Southern Empire will be just like home," Kai muttered as he fixed Junsu's lip. "But I don't really know anything about it and the people who are telling me don't either. People from the Southern Empire don't know anything about the Second Continent and vice versa. They all think they know, but I don't think anyone realizes what home is really like unless you live there."

Kai pulled his finger back with a sigh.

"Maybe one day the Southern Empire will feel like home," Junsu said with a hint of hope in his tone. "Not right away, but one day."

Kai smiled at his optimism. Then his expression changed.

"Do this." He pressed his own lips together, gesturing for Junsu to mirror him. The Alpha smacked his lips comically, drawing a giggle from Kai.

Soon, they both settled down. Kai remained standing over Junsu, watching him reach for the bottle of oil again. He lifted it to his nose and inhaled the familiar scent before trying to pour more of it onto his right hand with his nondominant left.

"Here." Kai gently hopped onto the table. He took Junsu's hands and placed them on his lap. He plucked up a bottle and poured a few drops of some oil mixture onto them. The oil smelled almost unbearably strong, but as Junsu's Omega mother used to say, that was how you knew it was working. The aroma of lavender, peppermint, tea tree, and eucalyptus filled the air between them as Kai lifted Junsu's hands and massaged them again, running his thumbs over each of his fingers and between swollen knuckles, pressing, caressing.

"I should probably...thank you." Kai whispered the words as if he'd never spoken them before. His head was lowered, eyes focused on Junsu's hands where his digits were smoothing over sore red skin.

"Should you?" Junsu asked. When Kai looked up at him, he smirked, drawing a huff and the reflection of a smile from the Omega.

Kai hummed a positive note. They sat together in silence for a long while and he kept rubbing Junsu's hands well past the point where the pain had faded away and the oil had been absorbed. He didn't let go.

"Kai?" Junsu whispered. The Omega had zoned out. He seemed tired and a little lost. "What's wrong?"

"I'm thinking," Kai replied. "Do you have an Omega back in the city? A mate or even...just someone you're with right now?"

Junsu opened and closed his mouth. He honestly didn't know how to answer. Technically Kai was soon to be his Omega, though he wasn't quite in the city yet and Junsu couldn't just come out with it like that. So, without dropping the charade, he answered as he would if he were the real Jaemin.

"No," Junsu chuckled, thinking of his friend, "I'm sort of what you'd call an eternal bachelor."

Kai laughed lightly along with him. "I can't imagine why. You're so—" He paused, once again lost in thought.

Junsu's gaze shifted. He eyed the shuddering rise and fall of the Omega's chest. Kai was giving off a light scent despite the suppressants and whatever other pheromone blockers he was wearing. They were so compatible, Junsu could smell his scent through all that nonsense, but the air around Kai seemed to be filled with a strange mix of uncertainty, confusion...and lust.

Ever so slowly, Kai moved from the table, but he did not stand. He kept his hold on Junsu's hands, kept them pressed in his lap. He slid down over the Alpha. Kai's knees spread over Junsu's thighs and slipped onto the chair on either side of his narrow hips.

He straddled Junsu, steadily resting himself fully in the Alpha's lap. The heat between his legs pressed over the answering bulge that had developed in Junsu's trousers.

"Kai..." Junsu groaned at the sensation as Kai pressed his weight down over him and started to roll his hips.

"What did you say your boss would do to you if he found us alone together? Like in the baths before? Like now?" Kai asked, his voice a breathy whisper hot in Junsu's ear. He leaned back and pressed himself down firmly. A naughty smile curled his lips.

Junsu couldn't stop himself from smiling back.

"Long walk. Short pier," he replied.

Kai moved in closer, so close that Junsu could feel his lips moving against his when he next spoke.

"Then this will be our little secret, won't it?"

Eight: Secrets

Junsu considered himself a controlled Alpha. He was not one to let biological urges or matters of the heart take over his mind and body. But being around Kai changed everything. Kai was the exception to every single rule Junsu had developed for himself over the years.

His control slipped further and further away with every grind of Kai's warmth against the front of his trousers. His closeness, his heat, his scent, the entire amalgamation that was Kai hit Junsu like a wave crashing into the cliffs, eroding his rock-solid reason and sending him tumbling down into the deep.

"Fuck," Junsu hissed, giving in to the sensation. His hands came up to land on the splay of Kai's hips, his thumbs dipping into the jut where his hips met his spread-open thighs.

Kai wore one of his purple matching short and top sets that day. The shirt was only held closed by two ties, a little bow at one side and one tucked inside at the other.

As Kai rocked against him, Junsu pulled the loose string to release one side of his top. It fell open, exposing part of Kai's chest and the pink peak of a nipple beautifully encircled by violet tattoos.

Kai stared down at him with a heavy hooded gaze. "You can feel it, too, can't you?" he whispered. Leaning forward, he pressed his forehead to Junsu's, still staring into the man's eyes while he rocked his hips. "We're compatible. Made for each other."

Junsu hissed out a breath as the slick of Kai's natural Omegan wetness began to soak through his trousers. Kai was so close and gasping against his lips as he dragged his lithe body back and forth over the press of Junsu's covered cock.

Junsu opened his eyes to meet Kai's gaze. They rocked together mindlessly, in time with their panting breaths. Then, without warning, Junsu gave in to the urge that had been boiling within him.

He arched forward and pressed his lips to Kai's. The kiss burned and tasted vaguely of ointment. It put pressure on his split lip, drawing out a pained hiss. He broke away with clenched teeth.

"Oh shit," Kai laughed, pressing his thumb to Junsu's bottom lip. "Did that hurt?"

Junsu grunted. Without responding, he turned his head and took Kai's thumb into his mouth. Moaning, he pressed his tongue hot along the pad of the digit.

Kai whimpered softly and his legs squeezed together around Junsu's thighs as he demonstrated what he could do with his talented tongue.

"Please," Kai whispered.

Junsu pulled back and waited for Kai to show him how much he wanted this.

Kai did not disappoint. With a deft hand, he reached across to the other tie holding his shirt closed and pulled it loose. The fabric fell away, slipping down his lean arms and pooling on the floor in a soft puddle of violet.

"Take me to bed," Kai breathed against his lips.

Junsu didn't hesitate. He inhaled a rough breath and leaned in to capture Kai's lips in a gentler heated kiss. He kicked back against the chair they were sitting in and stood. With ease, he lifted Kai into his strong arms. The chair groaned and nearly tipped over, but neither Junsu nor Kai looked back to care.

They were too busy consuming each other. Kai's hands found Junsu's jawline. He traced the sharp line of the Alpha's cheekbones before burying his fingers in the midnight-black strands of his hair.

"I can't believe," Kai whispered between kisses, "we're doing this."

"We're doing this," Junsu agreed. He stepped over to the bed, his hands sliding along the tattooed curve of Kai's spine and slipping down to cup the flesh of his ass over the little violet shorts he still wore.

"Let's get these off, shall we?" Junsu murmured. He pressed a peck to Kai's lips before lowering him down onto the edge of the bed.

Once there was some distance between them, Kai reached out and in one swift move he unbuckled and pulled away Junsu's belt. The leather cracked like a whip before Kai tossed it aside with a wide grin spread across his lips.

"These first," he suggested, hooking a finger into the Alpha's trousers.

Junsu grunted out a huff of a laugh but smirked down at Kai as he leaned back against the sheets, waiting with a raised brow. Junsu didn't need to be told twice. He kicked off his shoes and pulled away his socks before, with a teasing moment's hesitation, he started to unbutton his slacks. He worked at a deliberate pace, pulling the zip down one metal tooth at a time. When the zip reached its end, Junsu moved on to his shirt.

As he unbuttoned the soft white fabric, he couldn't help but chuckle at the impatient groan his striptease drew from Kai. The shirt eventually slipped away revealing a muscled expanse of skin. His entire body was sculpted and toned from his rough and tumble lifestyle.

Kai bit his bottom lip, but a moan still escaped. As soon as the shirt hit the ground, the pants were quick to follow. Kai's gaze was fixed on Junsu's cock where it was trying to force its way through the wine-red fabric of his underwear. Soon that slipped away and was tossed aside to the same forgotten corner as the belt.

Kai's eyes flashed with a lust Junsu had seen many times before, but for the first time the look made him burn hotter than a freshly unloaded barrel.

"Okay," Kai purred, spreading his legs in what looked like an unconscious move. His gaze never left the hard line of Junsu's cock. It jerked toward him, thick and wanting. Kai wanted it, too, if the growing patch of his natural Omegan slick darkening his shorts was anything to go by.

"Your turn," Junsu said with a smile. He was already leaning forward to finger the waistband of Kai's shorts and Kai was already arching his hips up off the bed to let him do it. The shorts slipped down the smooth line of Kai's thighs with ease and Junsu groaned as his gorgeous body was revealed in all its tattooed glory.

"You're a fucking piece of art, do you know that?" Junsu whispered because he couldn't stop the words from leaving his lips even if he'd tried.

Kai squeezed his legs together and looked away, a hot blush on his otherwise pale cheeks.

"Do you like my tattoos?" he asked, his shy gaze peering up from beneath dark lashes. "I've heard most Alphas in New America don't—"

"Fuck most Alphas," Junsu growled. He approached the bed, taking up the space between Kai's once more open legs. Gently, he caught Kai's neck in his hands, cupping the soft line of his jaw as they kissed again and again.

Slowly Junsu lowered them down onto the mattress. His weight fell heavily between Kai's thighs, pressing his rocking hips down into the bed. They moved against each other, thrust after thrust. The pleasure was driving them forward, but they both knew their bodies were aching for more.

"I want you," Kai breathed against Junsu's lips as their next kiss came to an end. "I want you, but you have to promise not to finish inside me. Okay?"

Junsu stared down into his soft gaze. Kai's brow was arched, and worry creased his features.

"Please? Fuck me."

Junsu pressed in close, inhaling the slight scent of nervousness slipping through the Omega pheromone blockers Kai was using.

"Kai," he started softly, "have you done this before?"

Kai sucked in a breath and shook his head. "Of course not. I'm not a slut," he scoffed.

Junsu chuckled at that and pressed a kiss to his lips. "In this day and age, I don't think anyone would consider you a slut for having a little fun."

Kai huffed. "You've not met my father."

Junsu hummed. "Well, let's do this gently then."

Before Kai could ask what Junsu meant by that, Junsu flipped his world upside down. He slipped his hands under the Omega's smaller body and rolled them over. Soon, Kai was lying across the muscular expanse of his chest, his palms pressing into Junsu's pectorals as he sat himself up.

Kai seemed to be about to express his shock at the new position when his body pressed back and Junsu's cock slipped between the spread of his cheeks. Instead of protest, a shiver racked Kai's body. He started rocking back against Junsu, letting the length of the Alpha's cock slide through the slick mess between his thighs again and again.

"That's it," Junsu groaned. He put a light pressure on Kai's hips and his grip rocked along to Kai's movements without forcing them. "You're in control, Kai. You're in control."

Something about those words had a clear effect on Kai. His next exhale came out as a heady moan. His hips stuttered and he arched his back, pressing down harder and harder, sliding faster than before with each delicious movement.

"You like that?" Junsu asked. Kai's head lolled back, and his neck arched forward. His eyes were half closed but fluttering slightly with each thrust. He seemed utterly dazed by the pleasure he was experiencing.

"Does that feel good?" Junsu went on.

"Yeah."

"You want more?"

Kai let out a high-pitched whine and nodded, his head bobbing with the rolling movement of his hips.

Junsu traced the jut of them with his thumbs, running soothing circles over Kai's tattooed skin. With soft touches and patient hands, he gently directed Kai's body.

"Sit up a bit for me, Kai. Yes. That's it. Come here."

Kai leaned forward until his chest touched Junsu's. A sensitive shudder ran through his body as their skin met. Kai was burning up; if it weren't for his suppressants, Junsu was certain he'd have dipped into a full-blown heat. Their obvious compatibility would have likely set him off and they'd be fucking through the rest of the week.

"Are you ready for me?" Junsu asked. His fingers traced the dips of Kai's spine, following the curve down to where it pointed between his cheeks. Junsu ran his palm along the design that curled its way over the plump flesh of Kai's ass. Following the lines with the tips of his fingers, Junsu slipped two digits down to trace his wet and waiting hole.

"I'm ready. I've never felt so... Please," Kai breathed, unable to complete a sentence. His voice was barely a gasp and he sounded delirious. He pressed the swell of his cock into Junsu's abdomen, rocking against him in search of any friction he could get.

"I want it," Kai repeated over and over.

"All right," Junsu whispered. He inhaled deeply, glad that Kai's scent was blocked. He was able to maintain some semblance of control without the lure of Kai's Omega scent urging his inner Alpha to rush things. "Stop moving for a second."

Junsu hadn't used a particularly commanding tone, but Kai stopped immediately. He was so intent on whatever was coming next, he didn't dare disobey.

"Please," he said. The heat of his words tickled the shell of Junsu's ear. His voice was a whisper, breathless and wanting.

Inciting shivers as he went, Junsu trailed long fingers down the line of Kai's spine. His digits found their place between the slick spread of his cheeks. Kai was wet and ready for him.

Kai let out a soft gasp as Junsu slipped easily inside him. His body shuddered as the thick length of Junsu's cock entered his hole. He buried himself deep with one steady thrust.

"Fuck," Kai hissed. He leaned into Junsu's shoulder, pressing his nose to his neck. He inhaled a deep breath, taking in Junsu's Alpha scent. His body calmed and his shuddering gasps for air gradually evened out.

Junsu closed his eyes. His hands were gripping Kai's hips, probably too tight, but he needed something to ground himself, to stop him from thrusting up with wild abandon. The feeling of Kai's heat wrapped around him was just too fucking good.

"Is this okay?" Junsu found his voice again, the words coming out as a husky growl.

Kai nodded against his neck as he pressed wet kisses to Junsu's skin.

"Yes. So good. More. Please."

Junsu let out a breathy laugh and his grip softened on Kai's hips.

"You're on top, Omega Yamaguchi," he drawled with a teasing smirk. "You can have whatever you like."

Junsu thought Kai might offer some huffing retort, but the Omega only purred, apparently too blissed out to fuss.

Kai slowly sat up and his hands moved from where he'd been gripping Junsu in a clinging embrace to rest on the muscled expanse of the Alpha's chest. His palms dragged pleasantly over Junsu's nipples before cherry blossom-tattooed fingers curled into his skin.

Using Junsu as leverage, Kai rocked back into his first thrust. A gasp escaped him as if it had been forced out by the pressure building inside his passion-filled body.

Junsu ran his hands up and down the inked expanse of Kai's thighs. He couldn't take his eyes off Kai as he moved slowly, visibly getting more and more comfortable with riding Junsu's cock. Soon, he was throwing himself back into every thrust. His head lolled down and his chin nearly touched his chest as he rode on, panting.

Resistance was becoming next to impossible for Junsu. Kai was tight and wet and perfect around him. Each slick slide shot tantalizing pleasure through his entire body. His glutes clenched and he plunged in deeper.

"Ah!" Kai cried out. "Jae—"

Without an ounce of hesitation, Junsu leaned up and captured Kai's lips in a kiss, cutting off his false name. He'd never hated the deception more, but the heat of the moment wasn't the time for such a big reveal. In the morning, he told himself before his mind faded back into the pleasure of their kiss. He'd tell Kai the truth in the morning.

In the morning...

For now, he lifted himself up off the bed and wrapped his arms around the man sitting in his lap. His fingers splayed over Kai's waist and around. His palms ran up and down the Omega's trembling back, gripping him, holding him close.

Dials turned on high inside them as the pace of their lovemaking increased. Kai threw his head back. He gripped Junsu's shoulders, bouncing in his lap until his movements turned erratic. A shuddering jolt and a single breathy cry erupted from Kai as his twitching length between his legs burst a trail of liquid heat between their bellies.

"Fuck me, fuck..." Kai gasped out as his thighs shook violently in the heat of his climax.

Junsu held him close as the waves of his orgasm washed over them. The creamy slick between Kai's legs made his thrusts glide as if he was pumping into satin. He almost forgot to pull out.

With a grunt, Junsu lifted Kai's still trembling body off his lap just enough to let the heavy weight of his cock slip away. His length slid between the mounds of Kai's cheeks and in that tight space, Junsu reached around and jerked himself off with Kai's slick lubricating the furious motions of his fist.

His orgasm was wet and messy. Junsu pressed his face into Kai's neck and breathed deep. He tried to pick up any Omegan scent. Kai's aroma was muted, but strong enough to send Junsu over the edge. He gripped the knot swelling at the base of his cock and tricked his body into thinking he was still encased in the tightness of an Omega's warmth as he came hard against Kai's lower back. The wet heat of it dripped down Kai's tailbone and into the mess they'd made of the bed.

Kai chuckled hot and breathless against his ear.

"Well, I'm glad you remembered to pull out," he murmured softly.

With a blissed-out grunt, Junsu fell back against the bed and Kai followed. He made no move to roll off his position on Junsu's chest and Junsu had no plans to move him. Kai's eyes were hooded, content and sated. Junsu couldn't stop himself from leaning forward and pressing a kiss to each cheek just below.

The pleased little hum this drew from Kai made Junsu smile.

"You're amazing," he whispered.

Kai closed his eyes and responded with an answering smirk before pressing a chaste kiss to Junsu's lips. When he pulled back, it was only to whisper, "I know."

Nine: In the Morning

Morning came too soon. Far too soon. The sun crested over the Pacific horizon and lit the bed with a warm dappled light, but as it rose higher it cast the room with a too-bright auric glow as if it wasn't the sun, but instead a nuclear bomb going off in the distance.

The shock wave would hit them soon enough. Rock the boat. Capsize.

Junsu had to tell Kai.

He'd been awake long before dawn, thinking of what to say. A burning in his stomach filled him with anxious dread that only soothed when he turned to the young man in his bed.

Kai was beautiful in the morning light, his face calm and smooth as he slept.

Junsu inhaled deeply, taking in the sweet smell radiating off Kai. The scent of flowers captured his senses as if the pink blossoms tattooed along the line of his neck were real. Without thinking, Junsu kissed each one of them and trailed his fingers along Kai's naked stomach, following the wave-like patterns that crawled up his torso.

Kai hummed a sleepy, but delighted sound. He arched back against Junsu's firm body, pressing them together. He woke in a moment of morning bliss and his dark eyes met Junsu's.

"Hey," Kai whispered in a voice lightly rasped from sleep.

Junsu didn't reply for a moment. Kai seemed to glow, his appearance so soft in the light haloing him as he rolled over onto his side. The sheets slipped further down his waist and Junsu couldn't turn away.

"Hey," he eventually replied with a soft hum as he cleared his throat. He smiled a sleepy smile down at Kai and reached out to move some hair off his brow. The black threads slid gently through his fingers.

"You're incredible," Junsu whispered, earning himself a little chuckle. "Seriously, you're really something else."

Kai looked up at him with a curious expression, his eyes narrowing slightly. "Meaning?" he drawled, teasing Junsu with dramatic annoyance in his tone.

Junsu let out a huffing laugh, unsure of what to say. "You're...you're so unlike any Omega I've ever met."

Kai snorted. "Wow," he huffed. "All right, I'll let the cliché slide, but you're gonna have to tell me how. How am I so unlike any Omega you've ever met?"

Junsu leaned back against the pillows as Kai curled up onto his chest. He looked up at Junsu with a quirked brow and questioning eyes. When Junsu took too long to answer, he ran one finger around the dip of the Alpha's neck and along his scent gland. The digit pressed there made the caress feel more like a knife to the throat.

"It's the tattoos for starters," Junsu said after a pause that was clearly too long for Kai.

"What, these?" Kai asked, tossing the sheets off his body completely, exposing his lean form and the ink that seemed to paint his entire body violet and pink. "It's traditional. Everyone in my family has them. Mine are just prettier than my brothers'. Kenichi has this awful warrior Alpha screaming on his back. It's terrifying. I don't know how he ever gets laid." Kai giggled and Junsu forced himself to hold back a laugh. Kenichi was a business partner after all.

"Well," Junsu went on. "You also smoke. You drink. You gamble—"

"Well," Kai imitated him in a mocking tone, cutting in before the Alpha could list *all* his many vices. "My parents let me do whatever I want." He paused, licking his lips and failing to hide the smirk twisting there. "As long as I don't fuck anyone. I was supposed to remain pure for my bonding ceremony, didn't you know?"

Junsu let out a groan that turned into a chuckle. "So, you're allowed to do whatever you want? You could be a little rebel because Mommy and Daddy don't give a shit about anything but your virginity?"

Kai shrugged. "Pretty much. It was our little trade-off."

Junsu shot him an amused side-eye. "At what part of the trade-off did fucking your bodyguard come in?"

Kai laughed out loud before burying his face against Junsu's chest. He let out a heady groan. "I guess I've spoiled the whole thing now, haven't I?"

Rolling away from Junsu, Kai sank back into the pillows. With sleep-glazed eyes, he stared up at the ceiling and let out a blissful hum.

"It was probably a mistake," Kai whispered thoughtfully. "But it was a really fucking good mistake." He turned his head and they grinned at each other.

Junsu's eyes trailed to the sharp line of Kai's features down to where he was biting his lip. Sucking in a breath, he forced himself to tear his gaze away.

"Kai, I have to tell you something."

"Well, tell me over breakfast!" Kai laughed, probably at Junsu's suddenly abashed appearance. He was irritatingly full of energy even though it was first thing in the morning. Still grinning, he pressed a kiss to Junsu's lips, crawled over him, and hopped out of bed wonderfully naked.

"Come on! Get up! I want us to go eat together and then afterward we can head down to the spa again. I want a full body massage, skin treatment, and a nice bath!" He pouted dramatically. "I really need it after the night you put me through."

With a soft exhale, Junsu cursed under his breath. Giving up on his confession for the moment, he climbed out of bed after Kai.

Already halfway across the room, Kai leaned over his drawers picking out an outfit. Junsu sidled up behind him and, with a smirk twisting his lips, he gently pinched Kai's sides, earning himself a surprised cry.

Kai slapped Junsu away from him in playful fashion and they both got dressed.

Not taking his eyes off Kai, Junsu slipped back into his clothes from the night before while Kai wrapped himself up in another one of his patterned top and shorts sets.

"I love these," Junsu said to him, tugging the loose short sleeve on his top. Kai's outfits were so unlike any Junsu had ever seen back home and very different from anything he had noticed any of the other Second Continent Omegas wearing. There was something both old-fashioned and youthful about the matching sets Kai wore. Junsu had been thinking about telling him how nice he looked for a long while, but it didn't seem appropriate to say anything considering the role he was playing.

"Aren't they the best?" Kai replied before pressing a kiss to his cheek. "Next time I'm back home, I'll get you a matching set."

Junsu sucked his teeth. Even though he'd been about to confess, to finally tell Kai who he really was, he found it so much easier to slip back into the little role he'd been playing the whole time.

"That would be telling, wouldn't it," he muttered. "You and Junsu's bodyguard having matching outfits?"

Kai turned to him, half dressed and pouting. He looked like an indignant child: arms crossed over his chest, brows arched. "It's not like Junsu and I are in love or anything. Arranged marriage, remember?" He waved away any worry. "Trust me, it won't matter as much as you'd think. I'm already planning to take this cruise home every so often to visit my family. If Junsu is anything like my brothers, he'll be too busy with Empire business to come every time and I'll request you as my personal bodyguard." Kai grinned as he tapped a finger to Junsu's nose, drawing a huff from the Alpha.

"I doubt he'll be as busy as you think."

Despite the tense conversation, they left the room with matching smiles though Junsu knew his was more forced than sincere. As they stepped out into the hall, Junsu promised himself they'd have the talk at breakfast. With that decided, he was about to put his arm around Kai's waist when a cheery shout from the other end of the deck gave him pause.

"Kai! I thought I recognized you! Good morning! I didn't know your room was so close to— Oh!"

Junsu sucked in a breath and froze. His heart both stopped in his chest and pounded ten times faster. Fuck. He recognized that voice. He'd recognize that voice anywhere. Pressing back against the door, he regretted letting it close behind him. *Damn automatic locks...*

Not three meters ahead of them, Lin Wesa stepped around a corner and came down the hall, walking toward Kai but staring Junsu right in the face. With each step, Junsu's world shuddered, cracks grew, edging closer and closer to breaking.

"Lin! Good morning," Kai said. He rubbed the back of his neck, clearly apprehensive to be spotted coming out of his room with an Alpha. "Um, we were just heading to breakfast."

"I can see that. I didn't know you were here!" Lin said with a big smile even as he frowned. He pointed back and forth between the two of them, stopping on Junsu. "Kai, I thought you said you two hadn't met."

Kai looked back over his shoulder at Junsu. He must have seen the oddly blank expression on Junsu's face and turned back to Lin with knit brows.

"I don't understand what you mean. Jaemin and I—"

"Jaemin?" Lin said the name slowly. His black eyes were focused on Junsu, shooting a dark look in his direction. "Who exactly is Jaemin?"

"I—"

"He—"

Kai seemed confused and he started to answer at the same time as Junsu, but they were both cut off when another much more boisterous figure appeared right behind Lin.

"I'll be damned. Is that Junsu Sun?" The already tense air turned to ice as soon as the name came out. Dom

Wesa sauntered around the corner, grinning as he trailed behind Lin, oblivious to the developing tension. Only when he came up next to Lin did the smile slowly fade from his lips. He stopped abruptly as if he'd just walked into a stone wall.

"Surprised to see you here. Small world, huh?" Dom chuckled, clearly trying to ease the tension. He looked at Lin, shooting him a frown, but he didn't get any response. Lin was too busy shifting between staring at Kai with a look of concern and glaring daggers at Junsu.

Dom followed his gaze and snapped his fingers.

"Kaito Yamaguchi, right? I recognize you from your photos at the house," he said suddenly, extending a hand to introduce himself. "Dominik Wesa, Alpha of Luxor City's Central Empire. We were just meeting with your brother, Kenichi, last week, but you weren't around the family residence. Away on one last big night out with friends before your conjugal banishment to Luxor City, huh?" he teased without reading the room.

Kai didn't shake his hand. He blinked at it as if it were a foreign object. They'd just been having an idle morning chat before Dom and Lin showed up, but Kai suddenly seemed unable to produce anything like small talk at that moment. He looked away from Dom's hand and turned to Junsu.

"Why did he call you that?" he asked. His voice was soft, almost inaudible.

"What? Junsu? Sorry, I guess *Alpha Sun* is more formal, isn't it?" Dom said helpfully with a confused laugh. "No need to play around, you two. Lin already told me everything. He's terrible at keeping secrets from me. Aren't you, darling? I know it's not official yet, but congratulations are in order!"

Kai was completely still. He just kept staring at Junsu, his eyes glazed over, lost and sad, but mostly utterly betrayed.

"Kai?" Lin uttered gently. He'd clearly realized what was going on though Junsu was sure he would have no idea how this deception had happened.

Junsu sucked in a breath. Lin and Dom's presence faded into white noise as he turned to Kai.

"Kai, listen, I'm sorry. I was going to—"

He didn't get the chance to finish. Kai was shaking his head, backing away. The young Omega then turned and broke off into a rush down the hall.

"Kai, please just—!" Junsu called out, but it was too late. Kai had turned the corner and was out of sight.

"I—I'll go after him," Lin said. He patted Dom's chest and sent a dark look Junsu's way before rushing off after Kai.

Dom stared after Lin as he left. With pursed lips he turned to his old Southern rival. The low wolf whistle he let out was like a bomb dropping.

"So, you really fucked up, huh?" Dom drawled. Having come around the corner a fraction too late, he was obviously still slightly behind on what inexplicable thing Junsu could have done to earn such a sharp look from someone as gentle as Lin.

Junsu ran a hand over his face and groaned.

"God, where do I even start...?"

*

Stupid. Stupid.

Kai rubbed his eyes furiously as he walked down the halls, heading deeper into the ship. His entire body burned white hot. Rage set his nerves on fire. He could hear footsteps coming behind him and he walked faster. He wasn't going to let that asshole see his tears.

"Kai!"

The worried tone of Lin's voice drew him to a stop. He didn't even know Lin very well at all, but his entire world had just been flipped upside down and in the middle of this vast ocean of lies Lin seemed to be the only rock he could cling to. So, Kai stood still and waited as Lin rushed forward.

"Kai, what happened?" Lin asked softly. "I just want to understand what's going on with you and Junsu?"

Kai let out a furious huff of laughter. "And you think *I* know? Isn't it obvious?"

Lin stepped closer to him, speaking gently still. "Kai, you can talk to me."

"If you really want to know, I'll tell you," Kai sniffed, still trying to hold back tears. He knew his face must be beet red and if anyone could see past the badly glued together mask of emotions he was trying to hold in place, it would be another Omega like Lin. "What happened is the man who I'm supposed to be spending the rest of my life with decided it would be funny to make me look and feel like a complete idiot! God knows how many people on this ship know who he really is! And to think I was really falling for—" Kai's voice shook as it softened to a silent whisper.

"Oh, Kai—" Lin started softly.

"Stop," Kai cut into his whispered coddling and took a step back. "I don't want you feeling sorry for me. I should have known better. You were right. I should have just looked him up. I was being stupid and childish, and I just wanted to pretend like none of this was happening. Like I had some kind of—" he sucked in a breath, searching for the word "—control."

Lin pursed his lips, casting Kai a sympathetic gaze. He quickly shot a glance over one shoulder, back the way they'd come, before turning back to Kai. "Look, maybe it's best we go back. You two clearly need to talk. We should find Junsu and have him explain what he was thinking—"

The name set Kai off. The embarrassment and sadness gave way, boiled up and burst out. He was seething. His face was hot, and he was sure there were tears streaming down his cheeks now.

"No! Fuck Junsu Sun! The sooner I get off this damned boat, the sooner I get away from that asshole!"

Kai turned from Lin and stormed off, continuing his mad dash deep into the ship.

"Kai!" Lin called, hurrying after him.

Kai was headed for the crew areas, past signs clearly forbidding all passenger entry. But that didn't stop him, and Lin followed close behind.

He swerved through the halls, trying to lose the other Omega in the ship's winding back corridors. Lin's footsteps became faint and his worried cries were muted by the ship's narrow halls.

Kai eventually slowed his pace but kept going. He sniffed and miserably walked past the dim back rooms and barren metal walls. He was rubbing his eyes when he next turned a corner. With a thud he ran sharply into a broad, soft surface.

"What the—?"

Kai looked up in time to see a horrible ugly sneer and dark eyes glaring back at him.

"Oh. You assholes," he hissed.

*

"What exactly did you do?" Dom drawled.

They'd ended up at the bar on the sundeck. Junsu sat with his elbows on the table, face in his palms. They were sitting near a buffet station that was still serving breakfast. The sun was flying high, nearing noon, and the place was not nearly as busy as it had been in the earlier part of the morning.

The food was about to be taken away, but neither of them was in the mood for breakfast. And it was clear that all Dom wanted was a good stiff drink.

"So," Junsu said, "Kai came on board and he was such an infuriatingly spoiled brat. I just wanted to play a trick on him but—"

As soon as Junsu started explaining what had happened, Dom raised a hand and stopped him midsentence. He'd waved over a waiter and ordered a glass of whisky to the table. Casting a glance Junsu's way, he made it two.

"You know, this whole event really isn't doing anything for my efforts to cut back," Dom muttered as he accepted two fingers of vintage scotch in a crystal glass. He gestured at Junsu to finish up his story. "Okay, continue."

Junsu sighed and went on. He started from the beginning, explaining the unexpected engagement and what he was doing on the cruise in the first place.

"My mother thought it would be a good idea to meet Kai on this trip. She told me it would be a nice, relaxing place to get to know each other, but when Kai first came aboard, he was acting like...well, like I said before. And he clearly didn't recognize me so I just...I'm an idiot. I thought it would be funny to tease him." Junsu sighed heavily as he confessed. "I told him my name was Jaemin Yi, and I pretended I was some bodyguard hired to protect him. We got the whole crew involved and it was as if 'Junsu Sun' wasn't even onboard."

Dom nodded slowly. "So, you thought it would be funny to reveal that Kaito Yamaguchi had been bossing his mate-to-be around the entire time? And you didn't see how this could in any way backfire on you?" He chuckled into his glass. "Not bad actually. It probably would have been funny...if you hadn't fucked him."

Junsu groaned. Of course, it didn't take much for Dom to put two and two together.

"Would have been," he repeated, cringing. He didn't know if that was true at all anymore. At what point would stopping the charade have been funny? He still didn't know and that's how he'd gotten into this mess. "God, I really shouldn't have let it go so far. I just didn't want to spoil the mood. We had something. We really did. I was beginning to think—"

"Well, that's obviously not true," Dom cut in, blunt as ever. "You clearly weren't thinking at all, not with anything but your cock at least." With a heavy sigh, he shrugged and took another sip of his drink. "You know, Sun, what's done is done. If you're lucky he'll forgive you and you'll get whatever that something was back. I mean, technically he should be happy to know he didn't cheat on his future Alpha before he even met him. Does it even count as cheating if you haven't met?"

Junsu didn't answer. He simply dropped his head and groaned.

"I fucked up."

Leaning across the table, Dom patted one of his sagging shoulders with the hand not cradling his whisky. "You did."

Junsu shot him a sour look and opened his mouth to criticize him for being less than helpful, but Dom simply shrugged and took another sip of his drink.

"Hey, look on the bright side, you definitely got to know your future Omega," he said with a lecherous wink.

"Not helpful," Junsu huffed and shook his head. "And he's only my future Omega if he accepts me after this, which I seriously doubt. As soon as we dock, I'm pretty sure he's going to get on the first boat back to the Eastern Capital. He'll tell his mother, who will tell my mother, and I'll—" Junsu leaned his head against his palm and turned to stare out over the water with a long low groan. "I'll just throw myself overboard. It'll be better that way."

Dom sighed and downed the rest of his scotch. He set the glass aside before grabbing both of Junsu's shoulders this time. He quite literally tried to shake him out of his dark mood.

"Sun. You just need to relax. It'll all sort itself out. There's still, what, two days left of this trip? I'm sure Lin is talking to Kai as we speak. Lin's good with people." Hearing that, Junsu let out a despondent grunt, but Dom went on. "You'll see. I'm sure he'll convince Kai to calm down and come back."

"Yeah," Junsu sighed. For the first time he looked down at the drink that had been poured for him earlier. With a shaky hand he took up the glass and knocked it back.

Dom watched him, patting his shoulder one last time before leaning back in his seat. He pursed his lips and stared straight ahead while Junsu drowned his sorrows, until a familiar face came running up to them.

"Lin!" he said, brightening up for a second before his expression dropped. Something was wrong. "What happened?"

Lin came rushing over to their table, practically panting for breath. His brows were arched with worry, distress written clear across his features. "Dom! Junsu! It's Kai!"

Junsu sat up, pulled out of his slump by the worried edge in Lin's tone.

"What is it? Where is he?"

Lin shook his head. "I don't know. I was chasing after him and then he ducked into the staff halls. I followed, but then I saw some men. They seemed pissed and he was arguing with them about a card game or something? They said he cheated them out of their money last night. Then one of them grabbed him and...I think he knocked him out! I wanted to do something but I just— I—"

Dom reached out for Lin, calming him with a soft hushed tone. "Hey, hey. There was nothing you could do. It's better that you got away to come tell us."

"Where did it happen? Where did they take him?" Junsu cut in, already on his feet. He was frantic, his heart pounding in his ears. He didn't have time for Dom and Lin's moment of comfort. Kai was in trouble.

"I ran after that," Lin finished. "I didn't see where they went, but I think they dragged him into a service hall below decks."

"Where exactly?" Junsu was already headed for the stairs before Lin could even finish. Undeniable fury coursed through him. He knew exactly who Lin was talking about. He remembered the Alpha from the card game and what he'd said to Kai. If that Alpha laid as much as one finger on him, he wasn't going to get away with just a bruised cheek and a cracked skull this time.

"It was the floor below the spa," Lin replied, gesturing vaguely toward the steps he'd come up from. "There's nothing there but a few vending machines and the staff halls. There were signs that said 'do not enter' and 'staff only' but Kai just went past them and that's where those Alphas were hanging out. They definitely weren't part of the crew."

"Shit." Without another word, Junsu was heading to the spa at a lightning pace.

*

"Dom, we should go with him," Lin suggested, watching Junsu hurry away. He pressed a worried hand to one side of his Alpha's chest, just above his heart. "It might be dangerous."

"Very," Dom agreed with a nod. "Watch our backs?"

Lin nodded, earning himself a smile from Dom. He leaned down and pressed a kiss to Lin's lips before taking off after Junsu.

From where he was watching the exchange, Junsu stood waiting for them.

"You're both coming?"

"The Empires have united, my friend." Dom patted Junsu's back on their way down the stairs. "We're in this together. Let's go."

Ten: Below Deck

On the decks above, the staff were rushing about getting lunch started. Almost everyone aboard was in one of the dining rooms or hanging around the parts of the ship that served food and alcohol. Even if they'd finished with their meals, they'd most likely migrated to the poolside or the sundecks. No one was in the dimly lit halls deep below deck in the belly of the boat, not even the staff.

Lin led Junsu and Dom through the gloomy metal halls back to where he had last seen Kai. The journey led them through twists and turns and down into areas stocked with boxes that hadn't been used for anything but storage in years.

They traveled deeper into the ship. Junsu wasn't sure if they were ready for whoever they might encounter in its bowels, but he would take them head on if it meant getting Kai back safe.

"I saw the Alphas who took Kai right around here," Lin told them as they reached a strangely dark section of the corridor. The lights were never supposed to be turned off, not in any hallway onboard the ship. It was a safety thing, Junsu was sure of it. Even on the level where the dim bar and card club were located, lights still shone. But in this hall, on this particular morning, the walkways were nearly pitch black. The only illumination along their path came from the small circular windows lining one side of the hall. Foamy water brushed the glass with every sway. They were on the outer edge of the ship and only a comparably thin sheet of metal now separated them from the vast ocean beyond.

Junsu grimaced and walked on, but he avoided gazing out of those sea salt dusted windows.

At the end of the hall, a single door stood closed, but beneath it a very slim sliver of a glow cut across the dark floor.

"Lin, stay in the corner back behind here," Dom whispered as Junsu crept ahead of them. "Keep an eye out and watch the hall behind us."

Without a word, Lin nodded. He quietly moved back into a shadowed hiding place and all but completely disappeared into the dark.

Junsu and Dom approached the door, staying together as they stepped silently down the hall.

When they reached the threshold, the whispering sounds of men talking filtered through from inside. At least three distinct voices cut through the thick, reinforced metal in the ship's hull. They were all arguing about something, something Junsu couldn't quite catch. But as he pressed closer to the door, one phrase struck a chord.

"This wasn't part of the plan, Nam!"

Junsu's eyes widened. *Nam.* That was the name the Yamaguchi family had sent over from their surveillance of the Underground. Nam was the Second Continent collector, the one headed to Luxor City, the one who kidnapped Omegas.

Dom was able to read Junsu's expression, if his reaction was anything to go by. "Nam?" He mouthed the name that had caused Junsu to frown. "Do you know these guys?" he asked Junsu in a hushed tone.

Junsu nodded a curt gesture as they continued listening in.

A voice that must have been Nam's was now replying to his comrade in a harsh, bitter snap. "I wasn't just going to sit around and let this bitch talk at me for a second time! He already made me look like a complete ass at the card tables!"

"Shit, Nam, this is a huge risk. Don't you know who he is?"

"Of course, I know who he is! He's a fucking Yamaguchi!" Nam shouted in response. "It's fine! We'll take him and the rest of them and disappear into the city as soon as we're off the boat. Just like we planned."

"It's not fine! Fuck, Nam! You think people are just going to shrug off a Yamaguchi Omega going missing? He had bodyguards with him! Three of them."

"It's a fucking ship. They'll just assume he's avoiding them. He said he does it all the time during that fucking card game last night."

"Really? You think all three of these guys are just going to shrug it off when they don't see Kaito Yamaguchi for three days? Just that big one really gave us a beating!"

"Fuck him! Fuck them all! We'll go up there and take out the bodyguards one at a time! Throw them into the Pacific. By the time anyone realizes they're missing, we'll be off this fucking boat."

"God damn it, Nam! This is getting out of hand. We had the goods, why couldn't you just stick to the fucking plan!"

As the quarreling continued on the other side of the door, Junsu touched the cool metal. The well-greased service door opened easily. It slid to the side with little force as it would so that a trolley could be pushed through it. He and Dom slipped into the room without being noticed by the arguing men and closed the door behind them.

The room seemed to be a staff lounge of some kind. A nice place for the crew to take their breaks, though it obviously got little to no use on such a busy ship. Four large pillars ran from floor to ceiling and a counter that was being used to store boxes of cleaning supplies extended around the perimeter near the entrance. Junsu and Dom ducked behind it as soon as they entered.

Crouching low to avoid exposing himself to the men on the other side, Junsu peered around into the room with his shoulder pressed to the nearest pillar. He immediately spotted Kai and, after the snippets of arguing he'd heard, he wasn't surprised to see he wasn't the only person these men had trussed up in this dingy backroom.

Bound and gagged, at least another four Omegas like Kai were seated up against a nearby wall. They were all either unconscious or semiconscious. The expensive-looking clothes they were all dressed in wouldn't have looked out of place on the upper decks of the ship, but there was definitely something off about them. These were not rich, high-class Omegas kidnapped from their relaxing vacation as Kai had been. No. They all looked stricken and malnourished. How long had Nam kept these unfortunates drugged and tied up like this? How long had they been down below deck? How long had he had them even before then?

"Shit," Junsu hissed, ducking back down next to Dom. He nodded his head, gesturing for his fellow Alpha to sneak a look around the pillar. "These guys are part of the Underground," he whispered. "Those must be the Omegas they plan on trafficking into Luxor. I bet they're going to just walk right off the ship with the rest of the crowd when we disembark, these poor kids in tow."

"Wait. What?" Dom snapped in a hushed response. A frown creased his brow. "Did you say Underground? I heard about that group from Xijuan. The rehab center in my Empire took in a few Omegas. I thought your guys dealt with those fuckers weeks ago."

Junsu let out a heavy breath. "We thought we had. We'd been tracking them throughout the Southern Empire, infiltrating and dismantling their ring for months before we took them down. We got their leader and had pretty much flushed them out, but just this week we got information that someone in their circles from the Second Continent is planning to take over."

Dom tilted his head toward the wall. "This idiot?" he asked. "Nam?"

Junsu nodded. "And now they've got Kai."

"Well then, let's get them out of there."

Not one second later, a sharp echoing *bang* filled the room followed by a groaning shout.

Not one to waste words, Dom took a step around the pillar, revealing himself with a gun aimed right at the group in the center of the room. One of the three Underground gangsters was clutching a freshly bleeding arm and though they hadn't yet taken any bullets themselves the other two were staring at Dom with the same wide-eyed expression of dismay as their wounded companion. Their argument cut off abruptly and they all turned.

"Good morning, gentlemen," Dom said with a grin. He barely had time to dive back down when gunfire sounded off, filling the metal room with reverberations and sparks as the bullets impacted deep into the soft metal of the ship's walls.

"Fuck, Dominik! You're insane! Kai is over there!" Junsu shouted over the noise. There was no need to keep his voice down now and no amount of gunfire could keep him from giving Dom an earful. "You've been hanging around those psychopaths in the Northern Empire too much these days. Jimena Faraji has rubbed off on you!"

Dom simply leaned back against the bar and chuckled. He calmly flicked a button to release the Glock's magazine and did a quick check to see how many rounds were left in the gun he'd drawn from one of the holsters strapped around his chest beneath his suit jacket.

Junsu stared at him, his jaw sagging open. "You brought a gun on a pleasure cruise?" he demanded.

"You didn't?" Dom replied with a quirk of his brow.

Junsu shook his head. Dom was the very definition of a wildcard. First off, how did he even get a gun onboard? And secondly, who the fuck brings a gun on a cruise?

Dom reached into his other holster and passed his second weapon Junsu's way. He held the muzzle and shook the grip in Junsu's face.

"Come on, Sun. We haven't got all day here."

Junsu took the gun and cast Dom a warning glance. "Just watch where you're shooting. They have five Omegas over there and we cannot have them getting caught up in the crossfire."

Dom nodded and quirked his brow. "Of course."

They counted down their time to an attack, waiting for just the right moment. They crept around to opposite ends of the bar and Junsu held up *three-two-one* fingers before they both leaned out. The Underground Alphas didn't see them coming.

Dom and Junsu returned fire, careful not to aim at the group huddled in the corner. Junsu got the man closest to the kidnapped victims in the leg, causing the others to move away from him and thus the Omegas. The other two hid behind the pillar across from them, leaving their companion bleeding on the ground out in the open without a second thought.

As they ducked away, Dom stood to get a better shot at them. Junsu followed. He edged out of hiding and over to another counter. As he moved around it, he knew he'd eventually be able to make his way behind the pillar where the Underground Alphas were hiding.

Junsu reached the edge and leaned out. The traffickers were right in his eyeline, but when he moved to stand, it was clear they'd caught on. They were already aiming his way, shooting right down where he'd been leaning out before. Junsu ducked back until he heard Dom's gun fire off behind him. The other Alpha's shots drew the enemy fire away. While they were busy firing on Dom, Junsu again stood and shot at them.

He saw one man go down clutching his side. He hit the floor with a groan.

The last man remaining stared right at him. Junsu immediately recognized his crazed eyes. He was the raging maniac who'd insulted Kai at the card game last night. His jaw was still bruised from the punch Junsu had given him. This man had to be Nam; the profile fit like a glove.

Nam ducked behind the pillar out of sight for a moment. Neither Dom nor Junsu could see him, but they had him cornered. It was a small room, and they would have him completely corralled soon enough.

However, they weren't given the chance to inch forward. Nam stepped back into view and pointed his gun, not at Dom or Junsu, but rather at Kai's unconscious form. His body hung limp in Nam's arms, but the big man had no trouble holding the slight Omega up.

Junsu growled and made a move to lunge at Nam, but the Alpha's movements stopped him in his tracks.

"Drop it! I'll kill your little bitch!" Nam snapped. He pressed the barrel of his gun to Kai's head.

Junsu lowered his gun immediately and Dom followed suit.

Nam held Kai's body up with one arm, pressing his gun to the Omega's face. Cautiously, he walked between Dom and Junsu. There was nothing they could do as he turned. Backing away, he used Kai as a human shield to make his escape.

Nam's back pressed against the door and he moved awkwardly to slide it open while still keeping a hold on Kai and the gun in his hand. As he struggled, Junsu growled deep in his chest and made to approach, but Dom held out a hand.

"Don't," he said with a palm pressed to Junsu's chest. "He has nowhere to go. Let him leave."

Junsu gritted his teeth, but he remained with Dom as Nam backed out of the room with Kai still limp in his arms. Once outside, Nam kicked the door shut.

The metal closed like a curtain. In a sick sort of magic trick, Nam disappeared behind it with Kai. Junsu stood frozen, staring transfixed at the door while Dom checked to make sure the other Underground men were no longer a threat.

"We should wait," Dom murmured once he knew they were safe. "We'll catch him when he lets his guard down."

Junsu nodded. "You're right. He has nowhere to run. Later tonight we—"

A sound from beyond the metal door cut into Junsu's words. Seconds after Nam left, shouts echoed through the hall followed by the clamor of a struggle and then a single gunshot.

"Lin!"

Dom's shout echoed through Junsu, shaking him to his core. His heart thundered in his chest and despite Dom's earlier warnings, they both dashed forward and rushed out of the room.

In the hall, Lin was nowhere to be seen. Dom and Junsu rushed through the ship and back through the twisting halls below deck. They reached the light at the end of the tunnel and saw the commotion they'd only been able to hear the precursor to before.

Jaemin and Shik had arrived. The siblings arranged themselves in the corridor on either side of Nam, blocking his escape routes. Nam stood between the deck's railing and the entrance that led below into the ship. The Underground Alpha had dropped Kai to the ground where the fall seemed to have knocked some of his senses back into him.

With shaking limbs, Kai was trying to pick himself up off the floor while Shik struggled with Nam, gripping his gun-wielding hand firmly.

Blood stained the floor all around them. Shik's feet slipped in it as they grappled with Nam.

Jaemin had been shot. He crouched near Kai, pressing a hand to his own shoulder, holding a bleeding wound even as he tried to help the Omega to his feet.

In the midst of the chaos, Shik lost their hold on Nam. He kicked out and landed his heel against Shik's knee. With a sharp cry, Shik dropped to the ground and Nam regained control of his gun. Just as he was slipping his finger back against the trigger, the sound of a shot burst through the hall.

Junsu stood at the end of the threshold of the stairwell with his gun raised, pointed at Nam.

Seconds later, Nam's weapon clattered to the metal floor. Thankfully, it didn't go off. The man himself fell to his knees after it. He knelt there for a moment, red pooling at his stomach.

Shik knelt across from Nam, panting as they watched him teeter forward. Scrambling back, they moved out of the way as the big man tottered like a falling tree.

Shot and bloodied, Nam keeled over. His stomach hit the lower part of a railing and the momentum of his upper body tilted him over the edge of the ship. There was a metallic *thud* as his body hit the side of the boat, followed by the splash of his corpse plunging into the Pacific.

"I think that's the last of the Underground overboard, boss," Jaemin commented, even as he hissed from the pain in his arm.

Junsu rushed to him. On the way, he gave Shik a firm pat on the shoulder as he went to check on their brother.

"Shit, that's a lot of blood," Junsu hissed. "Did it hit an artery? Will you be okay?"

Jaemin made a face, not answering because it was pretty obvious with the blood slowly soaking through his shirt.

Junsu ripped off a piece of his own shirt and fashioned it into a tourniquet. He knotted it tight and wrapped it around Jaemin's arm several times until

Jaemin complained the bandage was causing more pain than the actual bullet wound.

"You'll live," Junsu sighed as he gave his handiwork a pat.

"I'll get him to the medical station. I saw it just across from the spa," Shik said, already moving to hoist their brother up.

"We should take these two as well."

Behind them, Dom came out of the hall, dragging the other two Underground Alphas by their arms. He laid them out on the deck of the ship, both injured, but still alive. "We're probably going to want to get them to talk about how they managed to kidnap and sneak four Omegas on board...and who helped them do it."

Junsu nodded, but his attention was now on Kai.

Kai had managed to hoist himself over to a wall and was now seated upright with his back against the cool metal. He still didn't seem to be all there. His head lolled down against his chest and he was clearly still fading in and out of consciousness.

"What did they do to you?" Junsu whispered. He was angry—at the Underground, yes, but mostly at himself. If he hadn't let the joke go so far; if he hadn't...

A hand landed on his shoulder, pulling him out of his thoughts.

Lin stood above him, staring down with a look of concern.

"Is he okay?" Lin asked. He slowly dropped down next to Junsu. "When I heard the first gunshots go off, I ran back and found your bodyguards."

Junsu nodded and placed a hand over the one on his shoulder. "Thank you, Lin."

In response, Lin smiled a sad sort of smile. He then turned from Junsu and leaned forward to check on Kai. With gentle hands he examined the other Omega, feeling his head before carefully opening one eye to inspect his pupils.

"He's not concussed. They gave him something," Lin told Junsu. "You should take him up to his room. He needs rest and water."

"I'll call security and we'll take care of this," Dom said from the other side of the deck. His phone was already in his hand and pressed to his ear. "You listen to Lin, Junsu. Go take care of Kai."

"Thank you." Junsu regarded both Lin and Dom with a grateful glance. "Thank you both."

With that said, Junsu lifted Kai into his arms. With all the care of a new lover, he carried him from the lower deck and back up to their rooms.

Eleven: The Real You

Junsu got more than a few sideways glances among other odd looks on the upper decks as he brought Kai back up to his room. Kai was limp and groaning, dangling from his arms in a half-lucid state. His breath came and went in calm, shuddering exhales against the side of Junsu's neck.

Junsu ignored all the eyes on them as he rushed through the halls. What would he even say to explain? Heatstroke? Too much sun? A gang of Second Continent kidnappers?

Junsu shook his head. He debated taking Kai to the medical room, but all Kai needed was rest and water. He was certain Lin was right about that.

Arriving at Kai's suite, Junsu all but kicked open the door before stepping into the room. The afternoon light poured in through the window and seemed to breathe life back into Kai's pale figure. After a few hours of rest, he came to in Junsu's arms.

*

Kai's dark eyes blinked open and narrowed in the light.

"What? What happened?" he whispered, looking around, confused and disoriented. He jerked briefly in

Junsu's arms, struggling against the unknown. Then, he took a deep breath. The scent of a familiar Alpha was a comfort, but the last thing he remembered was running away from that scent.

With a relenting sigh, Kai melted into the soft mattress as Junsu settled him back down onto the bed. Kai's tired, glassy gaze followed Junsu as he padded around the room.

Junsu slipped away to grab a glass bottle of water out of the fridge. He then helped Kai move until he was sitting up in bed, fluffing the pillows propping him up before he handed Kai the water.

"Drink."

Kai took it without a word and drank away the dizziness that had engulfed his senses. Water quenched his parched throat; he hadn't even realized how dehydrated he'd been.

"Thank you," he choked out after finishing the entire bottle in nearly one chug.

"Don't mention it," Junsu replied in a monotone.

They sat together in silence, both still in a haze after the day's events. It was good to have a moment to breathe.

With a deep inhale, Kai cleared his dry throat and eventually got his voice back.

"Those Alphas…" he started in a tone that was less hoarse than before.

"You don't have to worry about any of them anymore," Junsu replied before Kai could finish. "They've been taken care of."

Kai sighed and relief softened his tensed muscles. His jaw unclenched and he closed his eyes. "I shouldn't have taken off like that. I shouldn't have shouted at that Alpha. I was just so angry."

He thought back to what had happened that morning. He'd run from Junsu, from Lin, from everyone and everything. He'd run deep into the bowels of the ship before bumping into that disgusting Alpha in the hall. They'd argued about the card game, he remembered that much, but what had happened afterward was a blur.

"I didn't expect him to knock me out cold," Kai hissed. "Fucking psychopath."

Junsu's brow arched in an expression of either concern or sympathy. Kai could only guess. "Kai...do you know who those Alphas were?"

Pursing his lips, Kai cocked his head to one side. "They were the guys from cards the other night, weren't they? Some piece of shit losers."

Junsu sucked in a breath and his gaze shifted away.

"What?" Kai demanded. "What aren't you telling me? Do you know those assholes or something? They're not part of your gang, are they?"

"No." Junsu's gaze returned, and Kai's frown demanded a response. "Kai...they're traffickers from the Second Continent," he replied. His voice was low and edged with something Kai couldn't place and fury didn't seem strong enough. "Their leader, Nam, is the one who took you. They kidnap Omegas and keep them in illegal red-light district brothels. We got intel earlier this week that they were somewhere onboard, Nam and his goons, but we didn't know exactly what they looked like or who they were until this."

"Shit," Kai groaned, rubbing his hand over his face. There was a slight bruise on his upper cheekbone from the altercation that had occurred in the hall before he was knocked out and taken below decks. "Lin Wesa came after me," he whispered. He looked up into Junsu's gaze with unconcealed worry. "Was he okay? He wasn't taken. Nothing happened to him, right?"

Junsu shook his head. "Lin's fine. You're lucky. He's the one who told us where you went."

"Shit." Kai pinched the bridge of his nose. What if something had happened? God, he never would have been able to forgive himself.

He was holding off a headache; whatever Nam had given him to knock him out was hard on his system. The warmth radiating from Junsu helped, but even the token comfort from an Alpha couldn't assuage the pain pounding through Kai's head after everything that had happened.

Junsu rubbed his shoulder gently and took his empty water bottle before handing him a new one. Kai accepted it without a word and drank down half the bottle. With a heavy sigh, he turned away from Junsu. Outside the ocean was so calm, so far from the raging waves rolling around inside him.

"All the security makes sense now, I guess," Kai muttered, raking his fingers through his hair. "Though you weren't really security, were you...Junsu Sun?"

Junsu's gaze shifted downward. He stared at his own hands before clenching them into a ball as if praying.

Good. He can beg for forgiveness.

"Kai, I'm so sorry," Junsu started with clear and utter sincerity lacing his every word. "It was wrong and I... When I first met you, I just thought it would be funny to pretend to be something I wasn't. You were being so...you."

At that, Kai let out a huff, but he allowed Junsu to continue his apology.

"I let it go too far and I'm sorry. There's no excuse for what I did. I should have told you sooner."

Turning away from Junsu once more, Kai sniffed. He ran one finger around the top of his bottle, idly spinning the cap on and off. The ocean beyond the window was calm. He let his body calm with it.

Still, his anger cooled, and his features softened, but a sad frown took over.

"You made me feel like a fucking slut," Kai muttered without meeting Junsu's gaze. "Like I was the butt of some joke between you and your Alphas and everyone on this goddamn boat."

"Kai, I—"

"And you *took it too far*?" Kai repeated Junsu's words with added air quotes before laughing out loud without a hint of humor in his tone. "That's the understatement of the fucking year!"

Kai bit his lip to keep from shouting. He was already getting louder and louder. What he really wanted to do was scream.

But he didn't really care about the stupid prank. It didn't matter that Junsu had used a fake name or claimed to be his bodyguard. He just needed to know what was true and what wasn't.

He sucked in a deep breath. "Just tell me, did you mean everything you said last night or was it all just part of your little game too?" Kai asked the question in a calm and even tone. His dark, sad eyes peered up at Junsu, shining with tears he refused to shed.

"Kai." Gently, Junsu reached out and took Kai's hand in his. When he didn't resist, Junsu enclosed pale, tattooed fingers in the warmth of both palms. "I meant every word. I know what I did was a mistake, but I wouldn't take back a second of what we had. I got to know you, the real you. I would do things differently if I could, sure, but I don't regret it."

Kai laughed. Curious at Junsu's choice of words, he tilted his head. "The real me?"

Junsu let out a half-laugh of his own and shrugged. "Don't tell me for a second you wouldn't have acted differently if you knew it was *Junsu Sun*, your future Alpha, you were bossing around all week." He raised his brow. "Would you have demanded I carry your bags and teased me every chance you got?"

Kai pursed his lips and was about to protest when Junsu cut in again.

"Admit it," he drawled. "You would have been a completely different person."

"I would have," Kai snapped back, conceding just like Junsu wanted. Except, not one second later, he leaned in close and hissed, "I would have been a thousand times worse."

Matching smiles spread over their lips. Then they both let out a laugh and that laugh turned to many more. Just like that, the tension seemed to lift from their hearts and relief warmed the cold air between them.

*

As their laughter died down, Kai leaned back against the pillows, smiling a coy little smile. One corner of his lips tilted up and his cheek dimpled adorably. He extended his arm and, for a moment, Junsu thought he was gesturing to invite him into the bed. Then he realized Kai was simply handing him his empty water bottle.

"You're so good at taking care of me," Kai said once Junsu took the bottle and set it aside. "Of course, you should expect me to abuse your kindness...just a bit."

"Just a bit?" Junsu repeated as he leaned back in.

Kai nodded, biting his lip as if it could hide a naughty smile. "Not enough that you'll absolutely hate me and not enough to make you regret this arranged mating, but enough to satisfy my needs." He didn't pull back when Junsu came even closer, and he pressed in when their lips finally met for a kiss.

"I'll allow it," Junsu whispered against Kai's lips, his breath hot as they parted. "I'll enjoy taking care of you."

Kai's smile grew before Junsu pressed yet another kiss to his grinning lips.

Junsu crawled into bed and gently let his body settle over Kai's. The tension between them melted away into the past and all was forgiven with a kiss.

They inhaled, noses touching, lips wet and parted. The remembered passion from the night before came roaring back. They arched into each other, Alpha and Omega, polar opposites, magnetic, each drawing the other in. Even after only one night together, their bodies were so familiar.

Junsu had never felt this way before. Any fear that they might be incompatible disappeared in a puff of smoke. Happiness was a warm sensation flooding his chest. He held Kai close, so grateful the man in his arms was letting him near despite everything that had happened. Kai could have pushed him away, never wanting to speak to him again, but instead he indulged Junsu's wandering hands and ravenous lips.

Kai was clearly showing him mercy and Junsu readily expressed his gratitude through the passion of his kiss.

"Ah, Junsu," Kai gasped.

Junsu hummed a pleasured moan. "It's good to hear you say my name," he whispered, pressing his lips to Kai's ear as he spoke.

"It's good to know your name," Kai tittered in reply.

Junsu pressed a kiss to the shell of Kai's ear, whispering hotly, begging forgiveness. He wanted to apologize a thousand times.

Pulling back a little, Junsu pressed his forehead to Kai's. He inhaled deeply, breathing in the Omega's uniquely enticing scent.

Kai effused a sweetness Junsu had never noticed before. His scent was honied, as if he'd been tucked away eating red bean cake beneath the cherry blossom trees lining the waterways near the Yamaguchi family compound.

Junsu pulled back again, even further this time.

"What is it?" Kai whispered. His hands were on Junsu's neck, trying to bring him back in close.

"Kai," Junsu whispered, his voice deeper than before, choked up on the scent that exuded lush and virile from the Omega's pores. "You're in heat."

"No, that's impossible." Kai scoffed, shaking his head. He stared at Junsu with a cocked brow, as if he had gone insane. And maybe he had? Kai's scent made his heart race. The throb of blood pounding in his ears signaled the change in the air.

Junsu wanted nothing more than to press the lovely creature before him down into the mattress and ravish him until they were both rocking as one with the rolling waves of the ocean beyond the bedroom.

"You're in heat," Junsu repeated. "I'm sure of it. Can't you feel it?"

"I'm on suppressants," Kai muttered. He was clearly in denial. "I haven't been in heat since I was fourteen."

Junsu pressed his nose into the line of Kai's neck, breathing him in again. If he was on suppressants, the drugs weren't working. Kai was ripe.

"Stop that," Kai groaned, batting him away gently. "I'm not in heat."

Junsu pulled away as asked, but he did have to wonder, "Can you scent me?"

Kai looked away, chewing on his bottom lip.

"You can, can't you?" Junsu chuckled. "You couldn't before but you can now, right?"

The moan Kai let out in response to his question was erotic to say the least.

"Why is this happening?" he whined, breathing through his mouth. He was clearly trying to stop Junsu's scent from triggering his heat any quicker, but it was far too late for that.

"Maybe it was what they gave you. Maybe it reacted with your pill." Junsu pulled back abruptly, shaking his head. "I should go." Kai's scent was too much. If he stayed any longer, they would end up doing something they both regretted, he just knew it.

"No." Kai gripped his wrist before he could get up off the bed. "Stay."

Junsu blinked. "Are you sure?"

Kai let out an amused huff. He wasn't one to beg or plead, Junsu had only known him for a few days, but he definitely knew that easy submission wasn't in Kaito Yamaguchi's playbook. "I'm not so far gone, Junsu," he snapped. "Besides, it's not like it's our first time. If I am in heat, I don't want to go through it alone."

Junsu settled back into bed and nodded.

"I'd rather not have this ruin the rest of my trip. I want to spend my heat with you," Kai whispered. His skin blushed so pink it nearly blended with the cherry blossom tattoos curling up his neck.

Junsu reached out, walking the tips of his fingers up along the path of falling flower petals.

"You want me?" he asked.

Kai inhaled a long, slow breath before nodding.

Without hesitation, Junsu tumbled back into Kai's arms. He held the small Omega close and inhaled again. Kai's scent was thrilling. A pleasured shiver ran down Junsu's spine.

"What do I smell like?" Kai asked as he carded his long fingers through the coiffed length of Junsu's hair.

"Sweet," Junsu all but growled. Kai's scent was more than sweet. Lush. Breathtaking. Erotic. Ready. But Junsu couldn't get that out. The scent triggered something primal in him, something beyond words.

Kai hummed in spite of Junsu's blunt answer. He pressed his nose into Junsu's neck and inhaled deeply. "You smell smoky," he whispered, "like roasted tea."

"Hm?"

"Surprised?"

"People have said I was sweet," Junsu muttered. As he spoke, he trailed his lips along Kai's neck, unwilling to break contact. He spread hot kisses over the skin where Kai's overactive mating gland blushed red. The sight of it drew Junsu in.

"Take your clothes off and touch me," Kai whispered, though his sultry tone still came out sounding like a command. "I'll make you smell sweet, Junsu."

Junsu's only response to that was to pull back from Kai's neck just enough to lean up and capture his lips in an impassioned kiss. He struggled out of his jacket and shirt, trying with all his might not to break the kiss as he stripped as instructed.

Kai laughed against his lips when one arm got caught in the sleeve of his jacket. He fell back into the pillows, chuckling to himself without taking his eyes off the Alpha.

Junsu tossed his jacket aside and pulled his shirt off overhead. The stretch of his torso showed he was the epitome of an Alpha, tall and strong. His broad chest tapered to a narrow waist and his abdomen rippled with muscle. As soon as the clothes were tossed aside, he moved in to press his weight down over Kai once more, only to be halted abruptly.

Kai drew back and pressed his fingers to Junsu's lips, blocking his attempt at a kiss.

"I said take off your clothes." Kai's eyes flashed down to the prominent bulge of Junsu's cock pressing through his trousers. "Those too."

With a growl, Junsu playfully nipped the tips of Kai's fingers. He pulled back again and shucked the rest of his clothes with a feral haste. It was a wonder he managed to keep from tearing the seams.

He stood before Kai, naked in the afternoon light.

With a pleased hum, Kai crawled to the edge of the bed. He reached out and his long delicate fingers wrapped enticingly around the girth of Junsu's cock.

His wide black eyes peered up, meeting Junsu's gaze as he pressed his tongue to the base of his cock and drew it up in a long swipe.

Junsu groaned. One hand left his side as he sought to bury his fingers in Kai's raven-black hair, but before he could pull the Omega in closer, Kai skittered away.

He moved back up the bed, a teasing smile spread over his lips.

Frowning, Junsu was about to growl at him to come back, but it soon became abundantly clear that Kai had plans of his own.

In the center of the bed, Kai untied the bows holding his shirt closed and let the patterned fabric fall open to frame his chest as he stripped out of his shorts. Beautifully naked, the tattooed expanse of his skin was all the more vibrant in the light of day.

Junsu couldn't tear his eyes off Kai as he turned away from him. He pressed his upper body into the bed and raised his hips high before letting his knees part wide. He presented for his Alpha in the traditional position, one most Omegas knew instinctively and often fell into during their heat. The position put his body on full display, open and aching.

Junsu sucked in a breath and shook his head. "No, not like this."

"Why not?" Kai asked, turning his head against the sheets. "Isn't this what all Alphas want? Easy access?" He let out a little laugh and spread his legs further, perking his ass higher into the air. He was wet, nearly dripping with slick, his heat clearly affecting him as a surge of hormones prepared his body to take the Alpha cock it knew was coming.

Junsu shook those thoughts from his head. "Kai, I don't want you to feel I'm…dominating you. I want it like before. It felt equal somehow."

With a groan, Kai lifted himself up onto his elbows. The effect arched his back further, intensifying his inviting display. "What are you talking about? Equal? I thought you were my bodyguard."

Junsu raised a brow. "How did you see it then?"

"Oh." Kai huffed out a laugh. "I was far, far above you."

Junsu groaned, his memory instantly providing images of Kai in his lap, bouncing on his cock, very much proving how on top he'd been that night.

"So," Junsu drawled, edging closer to Kai. "This is my turn?"

Kai bit his lip and raised a cheeky brow.

"You can see it like that if you'd like." With that said, he turned away and arched his back ever so slightly more. A clear pearl of slick slid down the inside of one thigh.

"Fuck." Junsu was beyond resisting.

Junsu knelt on the bed, his thick thighs brushing along the outside edges of Kai's long ink-marked legs. He hovered above Kai. His hands found his sides and smoothly caressed the tattooed expanse of his ribcage all the way to his hips.

In a rough motion, Junsu pulled Kai back against his body. The soft slap of his hip meeting the flesh of Kai's rear had them both moaning. It was just a precursor of the noise they'd be making until Kai's heat faded.

The Omega's warmth radiated off him and the wet slick soaked his cock where it was riding that line between Kai's luscious cheeks. Junsu palmed his ass and parted his flesh with his thumbs. He'd half expected Kai's tattoos to travel all the way to a painted flower around his hole.

"I'm in heat, Junsu. This is not a time to tease." Kai gasped as his body flushed red with warmth and shuddered furiously.

Junsu had never heard Kai sound so desperate. He half wondered if heat would be the one time he could make Kai say please, make him beg.

But he wasn't going to test those waters. Not yet.

Junsu leaned over Kai's back, enveloping him, skin against skin. In that position, he reached around. His fingers danced over Kai's chest, caressing the dips between his ribs that appeared when his back arched. The pink buds of his nipples were hard against Junsu's palms.

Kai gasped and rocked back against him. The rolling of his hips smoothed against Junsu's heavy cock where it rested between his cheeks, so close but not quite in position to thrust forward and enter him. Not yet.

"Junsu," Kai gritted out. He cast a savage glance back over one shoulder. If looks could kill…

"What do you want, Kai?"

"Junsu."

Their bodies were aligned, Junsu's chest to Kai's back. The heat radiating off Kai warmed them both. The pressure built, overwhelming the senses. Anticipation was palpable, swimming hot through the air.

Junsu, poised to enter, rubbed the head of his cock pressed against the slick entrance between Kai's legs. But he did not move forward.

"Tell me. What do you need?" he purred.

"Junsu Sun." A furious growl rumbled in Kai's chest. "I'll push you onto your back and ride your cock limp before you make me beg," he hissed with a venom that worked on Junsu like an aphrodisiac.

His cock twitched against Kai's ready body.

"All right then."

A strangled cry escaped Kai as Junsu slid so easily through the heat-induced mess pooling between his thighs.

He moved in for what felt like forever. Long, deep, and hard.

Kai's body was obscenely stretched around the girth of Junsu's thick Alpha cock. Junsu rolled his hips, drawing himself out to the tip before pounding back in. The salacious squeeze and the amount of slick dripping from his cock and balls had him grasping to maintain control over his need to fuck Kai with hot abandon.

There was nothing in his mind except pleasure and the want to satisfy his Omega.

Kai was shaking beneath him with every breath. He pressed back into Junsu's penetrating thrusts. Every time his Alpha's cock drove deep, Kai gasped and cried out. He refused to beg, but the way his body grasped at Junsu's, milking it for all it was worth, that was enough.

Junsu pressed a hand between Kai's shoulders, caressing the imagery painting his back in intricate violet patterns. Biting his lip, he sunk inside again and again. Kai was impossibly tight around him. In his heat, buried to the hilt, Junsu found paradise.

Kai cried out, more vocal than he'd been the night before. Shaking moans and soft whines erupted from him with every thrust. He lifted a fist to his lips, teeth sinking into his knuckles. He was clearly trying to hold back, but his heat was tearing the most erotic sounds from his lips.

"Ah, Junsu, I'm going to—" He didn't finish. He collapsed forward onto the bed. With one hand he reached back and sunk desperate fingers into Junsu's thigh, clawing at his skin.

Kai was shaking beneath him, his body burning up and shuddering in the heat of his ecstasy.

Junsu's thrusting slowed ever so gradually as he felt Kai's heat flex and tighten around his cock. He moved at a steady rhythm, fucking Kai through his orgasm.

Kai reached back with a trembling hand. He held Junsu, keeping him close, buried deep.

"I want you to..." Kai's fingers gripped harder. "Inside."

With a heady groan, Junsu's hard-fought rhythm broke. His pace went from steady to furious. Hard thrusts seemed to add to the heat inside Kai's body, melting through him. The sweat and slick coating the skin between their legs heightened the sound of every thrust.

As he toyed with Kai's body, his knot grew. He wasn't pulling out. Not this time.

A swell of pleasure burst as Junsu sunk in deep. His hands captured Kai's slim hips, pulling him in close as he could. Their bodies were soon locked together as Junsu knotted Kai. They had truly mated now. No lies. No unknowns. Alpha and Omega.

Kai came again around the girth of Junsu's knot. Over the course of his heat, he would many times. His orgasm was smaller but no less intense. He all but screamed into the sheets. Junsu could feel it as he filled Kai for the first time.

Bliss flowed over them, gentle and warm. Outside, the late-afternoon sun was shining bright and casting its rays over the shimmering blue of the ocean. The ship rocked softly through the waves in time with their evening breaths.

They were still locked together. Junsu lowered them both down to the mattress. He arranged Kai's heat-addled body comfortably in bed as he spooned gently behind him.

He pressed a kiss to the back of Kai's neck before drawing his mouth over his Omega's tattooed skin. His lips caressed each blossom lining Kai's throat.

"I hope you don't mind that I won't be a virgin on our bonding night," Kai whispered over one shoulder. Junsu smiled and Kai caught his lips in a teasing kiss.

Junsu chuckled once their kiss broke.

"Bonding night? That's an old term." He shook his head. The word was as archaic as the whole arrangement they'd been coerced into.

"Yes. Bonding night." Kai side-eyed him and for all intents and purposes seemed completely serious. "We're doing everything as per tradition according to my parents and your mother. Didn't she tell you?"

Junsu exhaled heavily. He stared up at the ceiling, half-hoping the sky would fall and swallow him up.

"She's always loved to play the enigma. What tradition?" he asked.

"As per tradition," Kai started filling him in, "we claim each other and bond the night after our ceremony."

"Why wait for the ceremony to bond?" Junsu replied with a wicked grin. His mother had planned for the bonding ceremony to take place after their arrival. Junsu didn't even know the exact date yet, another of Xijuan's surprises, but he did know that she planned to announce their engagement personally at a press conference once they disembarked in Luxor City.

He smirked as he let his fingers dance lightly over Kai's neck, tracing the pattern he imagined the flower petals painted across Kai's skin had fallen in.

Kai huffed out a laugh even as he arched into his touch, putting his neck on full display. "Our families will kill us." He whispered this as if said families were just outside their bedroom door listening in.

Hell, given their luck on the trip so far, he wouldn't have put it past Kazue Yamaguchi to have her son's room bugged.

Junsu huffed and shook his head. "They'll get over it."

With that said, he leaned back against the pillows, pulling Kai against his chest. Their lips were already on each other's necks, hot breath tickling the skin and teeth grazing over the heated location of their mating glands.

"Be mine?" Junsu whispered.

"What are you? A dollar store Valentine's Day card?" Kai pulled back to tease. Still, he pressed a kiss to Junsu's lips. With a luscious smirk spread across his still bliss-flushed features he replied, "I'm yours. As long as you're mine."

Junsu hummed his assent. "Yours."

Twelve: A Turn of Events

The cruise came to its inevitable end when the ship docked at the luxurious commercial port along the Southern Empire's western coast. The boat pulled up alongside the shining white façade and blew a single low tone to announce its arrival. The news about the incident that had happened on board had got out fast. That fact was obvious as soon as Junsu and Kai disembarked.

The neon colors of the Southern Empire's metropolitan brilliance couldn't dim the camera flashes blaring as soon as they stepped down the ramp. The red and blue of spinning police lights greeted them and, once the passengers had cleared the ramp, an entire armada of law enforcement officers scaled up into the ship toward the surviving members of the Underground. Only the captain of the force remained behind to shake hands with Junsu Sun.

It was a deliberate move on the police chief's part, a show of respect to the Sun Family in front of the press. Lights flared as the cameras caught the handshake.

For his part, Junsu Sun's portrait had been plastered above the mugshots of the Underground gang members across every newssheet and webpage. The Alpha of the

Southern Empire was once again hailed as a hero in Luxor City.

Every article about the incident exuded praise to Junsu for having dealt this final lasting blow to the illicit Underground traffickers who had plagued their back alleys for so long. From Luxor City all the way to the Second Continent, people were happy to see the Underground finally quashed through the efforts of the Southern heir.

The Sun Family couldn't have paid for better PR. When Junsu stepped away from the police captain out onto the walkway beyond the ramp, he was instantly surrounded by crowds of reporters. The newshawks had arrived to catch this latest scoop on the Underground traffickers. They all wanted an exclusive piece of the story's grand finale.

However, the headline they inevitably came away with was entirely unexpected.

The lead editors from all the gathered reporters' respective magazines had planned for a big news story about the rescue of a group of vulnerable Omegas and a great criminal takedown aboard a luxury cruise liner. They had a field day updating their headlines when the reports came in that Junsu Sun had stepped off the ship with Kaito Yamaguchi on his arm.

Screw the Underground. Junsu Sun's new Omega was the biggest story in Luxor.

The Underground feature turned into supplementary material. Phones were ringing and articles were already being scratched out and rewritten as Kai and Junsu approached the press.

So many questions came at once, they were barely audible. When had this started? Had anyone even known they were seeing each other?

Junsu held his head high, giving the cameras a clearer view of the mark marring his mating gland.

A bonding mark? Of course, it was. There'd never been a more obvious sign of a passionate night between Alpha and Omega. The salacious images of matching bonding marks would make for viral content for sure, and just in time for them to meet with Xijuan Sun before the press conference scheduled that evening.

Kai's hands were folded in front of him, resting delicately on the violet robe he wore that draped halfway down his thighs to rest on top of a pair of nearly skintight black pants.

Kai lowered his gaze demurely while cameras flashed. As an Omega from the Second Continent, he clearly had more reservations about this public affair than an Alpha like Junsu, though he did smile for the cameras. He even deigned to talk to a reporter or two. They drew him away from Junsu, waving their arms, desperate to capture Kai's attention.

Along the exit a stretch of the dock's walkway had been cordoned off to separate the press from the passengers. Kai approached the velvet ropes with an easy grace. The carefully embroidered violet silk clothing he wore clung to his lithe form. He made for a pretty picture, that was for sure.

*

Kai knew how to behave when he had to. He'd been well trained to put on a show for the press. Though, back home, his family had a stranglehold over the media. Any and all stories about the Yamaguchi Family were picked through with a fine-toothed comb, filtered and sieved before more often than not being censored completely.

His reputation in the media as the demure little Yamaguchi Omega from the Second Continent could only be compromised by those who wouldn't fucking dare.

As soon as he got near enough, members of the Luxor City press shoved cameras and microphones in his face, but Kai endured with a smile.

"What brings you to Luxor City, Omega Yamaguchi?" one reporter called out. His use of Kai's formal address was the only thing polite about him.

"I'm here to join the ranks of the Luxor City Lovers," Kai announced, giving the newshawks the sound bite they were all craving. He glanced to his right where Lin and Dom were passing through the crowds nearby and earned himself a little wink from the other Omega.

"Omega Yamaguchi!" Another reporter called out, drawing him down the line. "Sunita from *Luxor Fashion*."

"Nice to meet you, Sunita." Kai smiled politely in a way he was well aware would be picture perfect under a camera flash.

"A pleasure, Omega Yamaguchi! Welcome to Luxor! Now, this outfit you're wearing looks distinctly Southern made. Did Alpha Junsu Sun purchase it for you?"

"This?" Kai made a show of spreading his arms and casting his gaze down at his violet robes. "Yes, actually, it was my first gift from my Alpha."

"Who's the designer?"

"Oh," Kai hummed, feigning a thoughtful expression with his brows drawn toward each other. He tapped a finger to his lips, noting an aperture or two zoom in on the movement. "I'm not sure. You'd have to ask Junsu."

He turned and peered down the line of reporters. Junsu was not far away. He responded to Kai's gaze, as if he could feel it. Their eyes met and they shared a lingering glance until Junsu was pulled back into his conversation.

Kai smiled. "Yes. My Alpha would know."

*

Junsu held himself differently now that he was home. He felt the rigid, serious airs coming back to him as soon as he stepped off the boat. He had an image to maintain, after all. He wasn't some lovesick Alpha following his mate to the spa. He was the heir to the Southern Empire of Luxor City.

Still, when Kai looked over at him, Junsu couldn't help but soften and smile.

"Alpha Sun," a nearby reporter called out, pulling his attention back. "You have a meeting with your mother later today before her planned press conference in the entertainment district this evening. Is she expecting, well, any of this?"

Junsu's smile widened. "She is well aware of the fact that Kaito and I are engaged," he said, cheekily settling on a vague response.

The reporters murmured amongst one another. Junsu could see them tapping away at their phones, making notes, and murmuring into speakers. He had no doubt there would be a whole list of speculations spread about online within the hour.

"She knew you were engaged, but not that you two had bonded?" the same reporter asked, needing clarification for whatever he was writing down.

"Yes."

"When did the engagement start?"

"About a few weeks ago," Junsu said, soaking up their reactions with a hidden smirk.

The press frowned at the timelines they were trying to come up with.

One of them piped up again carefully. "And when did you first meet Omega Yamaguchi?"

"Only just recently." Junsu tilted his head back in the direction of the boat looming behind him. "On the cruise."

Again, the murmurs and questions erupted. This wasn't an announcement; this was a scandal! Junsu wouldn't deny it and he delighted at how every detail he left out added a layer of chaos to the unexpected turn of events.

His smile broadened. That was until a hand came to his attention. His gaze landed on a familiar face, one he'd seen at far too many of these press junkets.

"Aisha Kwon, from *Luxor Society*," the reporter said with a smarmy curl to her lips that made Junsu grit his teeth.

"Aisha," he greeted knowing already what was coming next.

"It's a pleasure as always, Alpha Sun. Now, there are many young and attractive Omegas from families within Luxor's high society and, from the rumors going around, you've previously been with quite a few of those within your own social circle. But you never took it so far as to bond with anyone despite the efforts of Luxor's most seductive Omegas."

Junsu raised a brow. Of course, Aisha knew all about those supposedly *seductive* Omegas. She'd made millions writing some of the most scandalous stories. There wasn't a single Omega in Junsu's *social circle* who hadn't had an Alpha help them through a heat only to be interviewed just days later by *Luxor Society*. You couldn't trust anyone when Aisha Kwon was handing out cash payouts for any scoop she could sink her spoon into.

With a polite smile, Aisha carried on. "So, what makes Kaito Yamaguchi so special, hm?"

Junsu's lips parted with an annoyed "tsk" and he was about to spit out a blithe answer when a warmth splayed along his lower back. A hand pressed against him, rubbing along the silken fabric of his suit jacket.

Junsu turned to see Kai at his side. He'd said his goodbyes to the reporters he'd been chatting with and returned to stand with Junsu. Kai's presence and the sweet rush of his scent filling Junsu's lungs was like a breath of fresh air.

With a smile, Junsu's gaze shifted away from Kai back to Aisha. He gave a one-word answer to her snide question.

What makes Kai so special?

"Everything."

To her credit, Aisha looked cautiously between the two of them and changed her line of questioning with a clipped haste. "Are either of you worried about what your families might have to say?" she asked, falling back on what was clearly one of her *safe* questions. "Both the Sun and the Yamaguchi families are known traditionalists."

Kai and Junsu turned to each other, and locked eyes. With matching smirks, they replied, "Of course not!"

In fact, Junsu could hardly wait to meet his mother for dinner. News travelled fast in a city like Luxor. He could practically see her fuming in the dark, her furious face illuminated by the blue light of a cell phone screen.

He had both spoiled his mother's exciting little media bombshell and done everything she'd asked him to do. He couldn't wait to see how she would grapple with that little paradox. It was going to be hilarious.

*

As the evening lights came on, Junsu and Kai dined in a fabulous establishment that overlooked the entertainment district's massive square. A maître d' greeted the couple with a flourish as soon as they entered.

"This way, Alpha Sun, Omega Yamaguchi." Smiling, she led them along the red-and-black carpeting between the shining lacquered tables. Overhead, globes of crystalline gold hung, dancing with light.

They passed through a red latticed doorway. A long table extended before the broad floor-to-ceiling window looking out over the prismatic lights of the city. At the far end of that table was more than one familiar face.

Junsu stepped ahead of Kai as they walked to their seats. A wide grin spread across his lips.

"Hong! I thought you were going to meet us at the docks!"

"Hey, boss!" Hong grinned right back at Junsu and clasped his hand in hers. "Sorry I couldn't be there. I'm on duty tonight."

At that, the pointed sound of someone clearing their throat had them backing away from each other like soldiers standing at attention.

Xijuan Sun slowly stood from her seat at the head of the table. Her hooded eyes were on Junsu. The lack of expression present in them was a clear sign that she was beyond the coast of rage and drifting into even more dangerous waters.

"Mother," Junsu said, greeting Xijuan with a polite nod.

Xijuan's eyes stayed on him long and hard. For what felt like an ice age she glared, but then her cold stare shifted to Kaito. The way she melted was ominous.

"Kaito Yamaguchi," she intoned softly. With a gentle smile, she extended both her hands.

Kaito briefly shot Junsu a look before he approached. He took Xijuan's hands in his and bowed his head ever so slightly.

"A pleasure to meet you, Alpha Sun."

The chill hanging in the air warmed a bit as soon as they all sat down for dinner with Kaito on Xijuan's right and Junsu on her left. Hong, of course, didn't sit. She stood just behind Xijuan's right shoulder, her hands folded in front of her, eyes straight ahead.

Junsu had a hard time keeping it together at dinner later that evening. There was something hilarious about the way Kai was able to mask his true self with a subtle smirk plastered across gentle red lips. He had a remarkable ability to smooth out all his own rough edges when he needed to.

Xijuan Sun's gaze was calm, but in an eye of the storm sort of way. Junsu could practically see the angrily frothing waters creeping up the shoreline but he couldn't have cared less.

He stared right into his mother's eyes as he lifted Kai's hand from the table and pressed it to his lips.

Xijuan blinked and sucked in a breath. "Well," she uttered, forcing a smile after a long stretch of silence. "I am glad to see you two got to know each other." Her words were snide, but no amount of sarcasm could hinder Kai. His grin only grew with Junsu holding his hand.

"Yes, Alpha Sun," Kai replied, speaking to Xijuan. "It was an excellent idea on your part to have him join me on this cruise. Such a wonderful bonding experience."

Junsu bit the inside of his cheek to hold back a snorting laugh. He had to admit, he was a little surprised. Despite the mended emotions between them, he'd half expected Kai to tell his mother everything, how he hadn't been sent a picture, how he hadn't even known Junsu was going to be on the cruise, and how much of an asshole Junsu was for pulling the stunt he'd pulled.

But none of that ever came out. Kai was having far too much fun vexing Xijuan with his overt displays of affection. He even reached across the narrow table and placed his hand over Junsu's as he spoke.

"I honestly think it was love at first sight. The chemistry between us was undeniable. Remember, Junsu? That day we went to the spa?" Kai threw his head back and let out a playful laugh. "You had to try so desperately hard to keep your hands off me in the baths, didn't you? It was nearly a scandal."

In the process of taking a sip of rice wine, Junsu very nearly exploded into a coughing fit.

Xijuan raised a brow. "The baths?" she drawled.

Kai gave Junsu's hand a sympathetic pat. "Your son is very passionate, Alpha Sun. I could hardly resist."

"Hm." Xijuan's gaze shifted as she eyed Junsu narrowly. After a tense second that felt longer than it was, she sniffed dismissively and picked up her menu. "Please call me Xijuan, Kaito. We are family now."

Kai bowed his head slightly, smiling coyly. "Of course, Xijuan."

The waiter came, breaking the awkward tension hanging in the air and drawing their focus to the menus. The meals were set so he took their preferences and drink orders quickly and appetizers came out only moments later.

The food thankfully stifled conversation to things that could be said between bites. Their drinks were set in front of them followed quickly by the entrees.

As soon as the finely marbled steak was set down in front of her, Xijuan started to aggressively cut into it with a knife Junsu couldn't help but notice was very sharp. His mother spent the evening making snide comments about him while at the very same time complimenting Kaito.

"I heard there was quite the media frenzy on the docks. Xijuan seems to think you're the one responsible for this whole turn of events," Hong murmured to Junsu after dinner. They were on their way out of the door.

Junsu walked with Hong, filling her in on a few details that he wasn't keen to have reaching his mother's ears. He told her in brief about the little prank he'd pulled before moving on to the incident with Nam.

Hong asked after Shik, who was fine, and Jaemin, who was still recovering from being shot. Junsu had given them both some time off after what had happened.

"Sounds like they deserve it," Hong laughed. "You know, maybe I should have been there. I wouldn't have let that prank you pulled go on more than an hour."

Junsu laughed but smothered it so his mother wouldn't hear. Hong was a no-nonsense Alpha. If she'd been there with them, the prank would have been over before it could have even got rolling.

Down the hall just ahead of them, Xijuan had offered Kai her arm. She was walking him to the door, patting his hand gently as she spoke to him.

Junsu watched the exchange with a smirk.

They stepped outside as Xijuan's car was pulling up. Her driver stepped out and came around to grab the door.

"Right!" Xijuan said, turning to Junsu. "Now I have a press conference to get to. It's nearby but I'm loath to walk. You may take a car and see yourselves home if you'd like."

Junsu was about to thank his mother when Kai cut in.

"Oh!" he exclaimed, eyes wide with excitement. "I would like to walk around! Is it safe?"

"Of course, it's safe, my darling." Xijuan patted his hands. "You're part of the Sun family now. No one would dare lay a finger on you."

Kai turned to Junsu. "Can we?"

Junsu nodded goodbye to Hong before stepping forward. He took Kai's hand in his.

"We can walk around the square before we head home," he agreed. "Then I'll take you out in the morning to see the city in the day."

Kai grinned and a giddy sound escaped him before his shy façade fell back into place. He turned to Xijuan and bowed his head gently.

"Thank you, Xijuan. For everything."

"Yes, well," Xijuan's eyes narrowed on her son briefly before she smiled at Kai. "Have fun. Let's meet for lunch tomorrow. Despite this little turn of events, we still need to plan the ceremony."

"Yes, mother," Junsu said, though he was already pulling Kai away with him. "See you tomorrow then!"

*

Xijuan scowled after her son once Junsu and Kai turned away.

She shook her head, wondering what devious methods her boy had used to lure such an innocent Omega like Kai into a bond. She knew Kai's parents had expected a traditional affair, not this fucking scandal.

They were supposed to bond on their bonding night! The night after the ceremony! Not one week into their first meeting!

Xijuan sighed. Things could have been worse, she supposed. At least they liked each other. Apparently.

"Hong."

"Yes, Alpha Sun," Hong replied as she came to Xijuan's side. She placed a hand on the open car door, signaling to the driver that he could return to the front.

"I want you to follow them," Xijuan ordered gravely as she slipped into the back seat of the car. "Those Underground gangsters are like roaches. We can never be too careful. And make sure a car is ready to take them home. For all his excitement I'm sure Kaito is tired."

"Of course, Xijuan." Hong bowed her head. "Oh! And I hope the press conference goes well! Even if it's, uh, less of an unveiling and more of a hassle now."

Xijuan scoffed and Hong closed the door.

*

As they crossed the street, Junsu wrapped an arm around Kai's waist, pulling him in close. Together they strolled toward the center of the entertainment district's main square.

"My mother loves you," Junsu drawled, not even trying to hide the disbelief in his tone. "And she clearly thinks all this is my fault." As he spoke, he swooped down to nuzzle Kai's neck.

Kai purred in response and leaned even further into Junsu's side. "Of course, she does," he replied. "And it is all your fault. I was just too polite to tell her."

Junsu chuckled. "You are so good at that."

"At what?"

"Your polite little Omega act," he replied. "Playing pretend."

Kai let out a huff. "Coming from you, that's a high compliment."

Junsu stopped. With a dancer's flair he pulled Kai around, into his arms. They stood facing each other, beneath the glowing abstract sculpture in the center of the square. The cubic glass was vacillating between colors, lighting them in a warm violet glow.

Kai pouted, but the expression quickly cleared away when Junsu swept down and captured his lips. The kiss was quick but heated. In a rush, it broke, leaving a smile behind.

Pinching his bottom lip between his teeth, Kai lowered his gaze.

Junsu leaned into his ear. "Are you blushing?"

"Shut up."

Without warning, Junsu felt himself being pulled in. Kai's hands grasped the sides of his head, long fingers sinking into his hair as he took Junsu's breath away.

Unlike Junsu's kiss, Kai clearly had no intention of being chaste. He tilted his head and ran his tongue along Junsu's lips until they parted. Junsu could taste the sugary drink Kai'd been sipping through dinner as their mouths melded.

This time, when their kiss broke, they were both breathless.

"Take me home, Junsu Sun," Kai whispered against his lips.

Junsu smirked. "I thought you wanted to see the city a little."

"I live here now, don't I?"

With a short chuckle, Junsu pressed a quick peck to Kai's lips. "We'll walk around tomorrow then."

*

Thankfully, Hong, on Xijuan's orders, had been waiting on the other side of the square keeping a lookout. With a cigarette between her lips, she was leaning back against the car she'd called to eventually take Junsu and Kai home.

Hong was having trouble with her lighter. With a grunt, she flicked it again and again until finally she got a flame. That flame was about a half inch away from the tip of her cigarette when Junsu and Kai came rushing up to her.

"Alpha Sun," she said, formal in front of Junsu's new Omega.

"This car's for us, right?" Junsu said, even as he already had a hand on the door, prying it open and hurrying Kai inside.

"It is, yeah," Hong answered. "Xijuan wanted me to see you home safe."

"Excellent, well, thank you, Hong. Good seeing you!"

"Goodnight, boss." Hong barely got her goodbye out before the door slammed behind Junsu. She stopped leaning against the side of the car as it disappeared out from under her.

"Don't worry about me! I'll just walk!" she shouted after them. Shaking her head, she took a drag off her cigarette as Kai and Junsu sped away into the night.

*

Junsu raised the blackout window between the backseat and the driver as soon as he'd finished telling the woman to take them home. He was sure she could still hear them, but these private drivers were very discreet.

Kai was halfway in his lap. The violet silk of his nice new outfit slipped off one shoulder as he moved himself against Junsu's body. In the confined space, the heat between them was already starting to fog up the windows.

"Kai, fuck." Junsu hissed as Kai's teeth sunk into his neck. It wasn't hard enough to set him off, but more than enough to get him going. "We'll be home in twenty minutes. There's a bed and everything," he teased.

Kai pulled back and pouted with his lips pursed dramatically. "You'd make your new mate wait twenty whole minutes?"

With a growl, Junsu leaned in and captured his pout. They moaned into each other's mouths, gasping hot and heavy as the kiss deepened.

"No one's ever made me feel the way you do," Kai whispered against Junsu's lips as they broke away from each other, gasping.

"Oh, how's that?" Junsu tucked his face into Kai's neck. He pressed delicate kisses and nips to his Omega's marked mating gland. At the same time, one hand slipped down over the fabric of Kai's now loose robes.

Kai let out a shuddering gasp. Junsu's hand trailed over his thigh, down to his knee, before slipping up again. His fingers dipped between Kai's legs and cupped the warm place between his thighs. That drew a shiver from him.

"Junsu," he breathed. His breath was coming out in heavy exhales as Junsu worked his fingers, curling them again and again, squeezing gently.

"How's that?" Junsu repeated his question from before with an altogether different meaning. He ground the heel of his palm into Kai while caressing the hard length of his cock, bulging through the fabric of his robes.

Kai let his head fall back against the seat as a long, heady moan escaped him. "You're so good to me, Alpha. Don't stop."

Junsu growled and increased the speed of his movements. He caressed Kai through the fabric of his clothes until he let out a choked cry. His hips thrust up and Junsu could feel his entire body shudder again and again.

Kai's head lolled to one side, falling onto Junsu's shoulder.

With Kai's breath hot on his neck, Junsu leaned back. He gave one final squeeze, before his hand left the now growing patch of wetness seeping through Kai's new clothes.

They only realized the car had stopped a few minutes later when the sound of the driver's side door closing resonated through the vehicle.

Junsu and Kai pulled away from each other.

"Well," Junsu drawled with a smirk, "ready to see your new home?"

Kai nodded.

They both climbed out of the car, neither of them even a bit bashful as they walked past their high-strung driver. She was sitting on the hood of the car, smoking a cigarette.

Junsu half turned to her as they passed. He paused. "Vanna, isn't it?" he asked.

The driver, Vanna, took a long drag on her cigarette before answering. "Yup," she said, popping the p.

"Ah, well, thank you for the lift."

Vanna's eyes flashed between Junsu and Kai. "Of course, Alpha Sun. Sorry, I didn't notify you when we arrived. You two seemed...occupied."

Kai snorted out a laugh, turned from Vanna, and walked up to his new home.

Junsu forced a smile. "Right. Well. Goodnight."

Vanna grunted out something that could barely be described as a response and took another drag of her cigarette.

Junsu huffed to himself. He hid his amusement by turning around and walking away to meet Kai at the door.

"It looks kind of small," Kai murmured as he took in Junsu's glass mansion. "I suppose I can't see much of it right now. Is there water nearby? Anyway, I'm sure it's all much more impressive in the daylight."

"Most things are," Junsu replied. He walked up to the door, keys in hand. He pressed the metal into the lock before turning to Kai. "You ready?"

"Junsu," Kai groaned, clearly done with the games. "Take me inside and finish what you started in the car or I'll be on the next boat back across the Pacific."

Junsu grinned, the lock clicked, and the door opened. "Shall we?"

*

Kai didn't take the time to truly appreciate his new home, but he was vaguely impressed by the clean white simplicity of the space. Junsu clearly wasn't a man who kept tat around.

With a hand pressed to Kai's lower back, Junsu swept him across the warm marble floors and into the living room. High floor-to-ceiling windows seemed to promise a magnificent view but were black as the night beyond them. Their reflections shone in the glass like a mirror into another world.

Kai caught sight of himself and paused. His hand was on Junsu's chest as his Alpha turned to face him. Junsu hadn't noticed the reflection's shifting gaze; he clearly only had eyes for Kai in that moment.

"We make a cute couple, don't we?" Kai murmured. He tilted his head back, admiring Junsu's mark on his neck. He didn't have long to appreciate it before Junsu bowed down to press his lips against Kai's collarbone, obscuring the reflection.

Junsu pressed desperate kisses over Kai's mark, tasting his Omega's skin. He backed them toward the couch. A hand slipped across Kai's upper chest, easing the shoulder of his robe away as they moved down onto the couch.

"You promised me a bed," Kai huffed. He tried to come off annoyed, but his little smirk gave him away. With grace their tryst hadn't had so far that night, he splayed himself across the soft fabric of the sofa, lounging back against one of the thick pillows near the arm.

"Can't wait," Junsu replied as he followed after Kai. He crawled over his Omega, watching his every move like a hungry animal. "Besides, look at the state you got me in. I can't safely get us upstairs like this." Junsu gestured down between his legs where *the state he was in* was prominent.

Kai snorted out a laugh and eyed the sight with a raised brow. His only response was a low hum.

He reached out and cupped Junsu's cock through his trousers. The warmth of his body had Kai biting his bottom lip. He'd gotten off in the car, but he was oh-so-ready to go again.

Junsu pressed himself over Kai and kissed his neck while working on the fastenings holding his violet robes together.

Kai lay back, just letting it happen. He arched up into Junsu's touch, tingling at every caress. The robe pulled smoothly away from the tattooed expanse of his torso and hung loose around his elbows where they were bent up near his head, hands resting graceful and listless near his temples.

"You're gorgeous," Junsu whispered.

Kai closed his eyes and hummed. "I know," he shot right back.

A second later, the imitation of demure tranquility broke with a shrill cry. Junsu grabbed Kai's hips in two large hands and pulled Kai's lower half into his lap. With his robes hanging off him, Kai was all but naked while Junsu was still wearing his suit.

"Unfair!"

"Oh, I'll show you unfair." Junsu's large hands released his hips only to come back around to grip his ass. He took two handfuls with a fleshy smack and squeezed.

"Jun!" Kai growled. Rock hard, his cock reached up to Junsu, pressing wet against his shirt. His hips rolled in Junsu's lap and he arched his body down against the straining bulge in his Alpha's trousers. "Fuck me."

With a growl of his own, Junsu pulled back. He made quick work of his clothes, stripping himself naked. He laid the weight of his body over Kai's once more. Hard lengths pressed into each other. Junsu ground down over Kai, thrusting against his slighter frame, mimicking movement they were both anticipating without providing the satisfaction of penetration. Not just yet.

Kai spread his legs as wide as he could and lifted his hips up to meet Junsu's downward thrusts. Their cocks moved against each other in a rough slide.

"Jun. Fuck." A strained gasp escaped Kai. His legs were shaking as the pleasure consumed him. He was coming close, nearing the point of no return, but he needed more.

As if reading his mind, Junsu slipped the length of his cock down. The enlarged red tip pressed against Kai, but Junsu merely tapped his hole before sliding lower down between his cheeks.

Kai felt him there, hot and thick between his legs. Junsu let out a groan as he rocked steadily between the beautifully tattooed flesh of Kai's ass. He passed over that needy place, wet and dripping, but every ounce of friction was just a tease. He didn't press forward, not yet.

The foreplay was agony.

Kai gritted his teeth and nearly screamed when Junsu again passed over where he needed him most without thrusting inside. The seductive tease had Kai moving his hips up to meet Junsu's cock. His muscles pulsed and he strained, up and up, over and over, trying to get more of anything his Alpha would give him.

"Junsu!"

A deep chuckle sounded in response to Kai's cries. Junsu leaned over him and covered his smaller Omegan body with his broad Alpha form. He pressed his lips to the shell of Kai's ear.

"I've been wanting to make you beg for a while now," Junsu whispered.

Kai's eyes shot open, narrow, but his gaze was too lust-heavy to carry any real rage.

"Junsu." Kai said his name again, but this time there was a hint of warning in his tone.

Junsu just smiled and pressed a kiss to Kai's neck. He shifted over him, coming to his knees. Kai was light as a feather and easy enough to pull into place. Tattooed hips slid up his thighs until Junsu's cock was lined up with the slick wet crease between Kai's legs.

He rocked, sliding forward along Kai's entrance. Once his balls hit Kai's shapely ass, he pulled back and did it again. The tip of his cock caught on the rim of Kai's hole for a second, pressing without entering. The pressure was so good, but then all too soon it was gone and Junsu slipped over him again and again.

Wonderful agony licked his skin on repeat. Kai arched back and groaned. All pretense was abandoned with a pleasured jolt.

"Please, Junsu! Just fuck me."

A chuckle rumbled between them.

"There it is." Junsu's whispered reply came out as if he were talking more to himself than to Kai.

Kai opened his eyes to check, but as soon as he did a force of pleasure rushed through him. A sharp cry escaped his lips, surging from his chest. He craned his neck back.

With a single thrust, Junsu's thick Alpha cock sunk through Kai's ready body. Junsu buried himself deep in a movement that seemed to go on forever.

Kai shuddered as the sensation tore through him. A token orgasm rushed out of him, small but powerful. His thighs shuddered where they were trying so hard to grip Junsu's waist and pull him in closer.

They stayed like that for a long while, their bodies connected, chest to chest. Silence filled the living room, and nothing but their sharp breaths filtered through the air.

Junsu groaned above him. "You look so good like this. Shaking under me."

Kai hadn't even noticed his eyes were closed. Pleasure was the only thing on his mind. When he opened them, he met Junsu's dark and hooded gaze.

"Shit, Kai," Junsu hissed. "You're beautiful."

Kai hummed his appreciation. He rolled his hips in Junsu's lap, pressing forward, seeking more.

Junsu didn't make him wait. He drove in and out of Kai as his smaller body contracted around Junsu's girth.

Kai could already feel another rush of pleasure building inside his chest. The flood of it swelled toward a shuddering climax.

They'd only known each other a few days but already Junsu knew how to work his body like a master craftsman. *Will every time be like this?* Kai could only hope so.

Kai pulled Junsu down over him and drew him close for a kiss. As their lips met, Junsu's pace sped up. He soon had Kai gasping into his mouth.

"Fuck," Kai whimpered softly. He clutched Junsu's shoulders, digging his nails in as the Alpha pounded his wet hole harder. The length of his cock filled Kai so deep he could feel the warm pressure of it burning hot in his abdomen.

All of a sudden, Junsu lifted Kai off the couch. He rolled them over until he sat with Kai in his lap. Kai leaned over him, shocked.

With a grunt, Junsu planted his feet on the floor and pressed up. His hips rolled. He was at the very edge of the couch, thrusting up over and over into Kai.

Kai collapsed forward with a moan. His hands slipped from Junsu's shoulders. Gripping the back of the couch, his knuckles white, he rocked against Junsu. They moved in tandem. Their bodies rolled like a great wave.

With Kai above him, Junsu had easy access to his tattooed torso. He pressed his lips to the pink nub of one nipple and rolled it against his tongue. His hands dragged up and down along the curve of Kai's spine while he lapped at every one of his Omega's erogenous zones.

Kai shuddered above him. Attacked on all sides by sensation and pleasure, his body couldn't take it anymore. His cock twitched between them, coming untouched in a wet spattering mess across Junsu's heaving stomach.

He cried out, but his Alpha didn't stop. If anything, his pleasurable onslaught on Kai's body surged as he fucked his Omega through his orgasm.

Kai collapsed onto Junsu. He buried his face in his Alpha's neck and gasped hot breaths against his mating mark as Junsu's rough thrusts continued.

With his hands gripping Kai's hips, Junsu pulled his Omega close. He growled. The way he moved was primal, as if he was no longer in control of himself.

Squeezing tight and thrusting deep, Junsu stilled beneath him. His hips arched up as he pulled Kai down into his lap. Their bodies were connected more closely than ever before.

Kai sucked in a breath. Another burst of pleasure coursed through him at the sensation of Junsu's thick knot pulsing inside him. It filled him perfectly. Warmth spread through his abdomen, a heady sensation that had him purring against Junsu's skin.

He ran his hands over his Alpha's chest. Corded muscles moved beneath his skin with every panting breath and sweat pooled wet along the centerline of his body.

"Well, if your plan is to fuck me over every horizontal surface in the house, that's one down," Kai murmured after the post-orgasmic bliss faded.

Junsu sucked in a deep breath and it came back out in a huff of laughter. He cupped the back of Kai's neck and pulled him in.

When their lazy kiss broke, Junsu whispered against Kai's lips, "I'll take you upstairs if you want to make it two."

Kai rolled his eyes, but when he opened his mouth to shoot back a witty reply all he got out was a sharp yelp. Junsu was on his feet all of a sudden and he'd scooped Kai up with him.

"To our bed?"

Kai warmed a little when Junsu asked that. *Our bed.*

He nodded his head before resting it softly against one of Junsu's broad shoulders. The smirking curl of his Alpha's smile was just barely visible.

Kai shifted in his arms just enough to press a chaste kiss to one twisting corner of his lips.

"Take me to our bed."

Junsu did just that.

Epilogue

The evening of the press conference, Xijuan walked out onto a small stage set up in the center of the Southern Empire's entertainment district square. Her appearance was met with a polite round of applause from the media and flashing lights as they snapped shots for their articles. Tonight, Xijuan Sun had a big announcement to make, an announcement she'd been keeping secret for weeks.

Though, by that evening, everyone already knew.

Despite the events of the day, Xijuan smiled and waved with her usual controlled calm. She stood at her podium, chin held high as she waited for the noise to die down.

"Members of the press, welcome. Now, I will be brief because we've all got better things to do on a Saturday night. I've asked you all here to share some important news regarding the Sun Family. As many of you now know and have seen my son has bonded."

The announcement was supposed to be met with murmurs and gasps and raised brows, but Xijuan didn't get any of that. The surprise had been sadly spoiled.

She sighed.

"The reason you are only hearing about this now...or rather today...is because this arrangement between my son, Junsu, and Kaito Yamaguchi is not just a bonding between Alpha and Omega, it is also a bonding between Luxor City and the Second Continent."

That raised some eyebrows. Xijuan pushed down a smile and went on with all seriousness in her tone.

"While I have no intention of stepping down anytime soon, to solidify the relationship between the Southern Empire and the Second Continent is integral to this Empire's future. The unification of Luxor City itself was just the first step. We are on the forefront to unify the globe. Partners like those we have in the Second Continent are indispensable. My heir and Omega Yamaguchi are bonding...*have* bonded...to set an example. Unions are fostered by the people, for the people and we must have everyone working together if we want to thrive.

"A single bad apple spoils the bunch." Xijuan grit her teeth because the metaphor was *tart* to say the least, but her speech writer had been very persistent about keeping it in. "The recent news about the end of an organization called the Underground should come as no surprise. In coordination with the Second Continent, we were able to hunt these villains down and put an end to their illicit activities. And so, I leave you with a warning. To any other *bad apples* out there, know this, if you continue on as you are, you will rot and the acrid stench you exude will lead us right to you."

With that threat hanging in the air, the speech came to an end and Xijuan waited for her applause to fade before taking a deep breath.

"Now," she drawled, "are there any questions?"

The words had barely passed her lips before an eruption of noise filled the once-calm evening air. The press were on their feet. Hands shot up. Questions were coming one over the other as every single person below the pulpit cried out, vying for attention.

Xijuan sighed. She supposed she'd brought this on herself. The big reveal would have been a lot more fun, if Junsu hadn't ruined it. Rolling her eyes, Xijuan decided to let him have this little piece of payback. He'd done everything she'd asked, after all.

As she took the first of many questions from the press, Xijuan knew it was going to be a long night.

*

Junsu stood barefoot in the open patio doorway surrounded by the floor-to-ceiling walls of glass that encompassed his home. Glowing in the morning light, the ocean roared far away from his peaceful piece of tranquility. He sipped a delicate cup of white tea as the gentle remnants of those great waves rolled up onto the beach surrounding his property.

This had always been his favorite spot in the house, his favorite view, but something about it now felt even more serene. He'd never been so at peace.

A soft meow caught his attention.

"Yes, Jun's so mean, isn't he? Not feeding you before he enjoys his tea."

Kai's voice followed by another meow of supposed agreement sounded behind Junsu, drawing his gaze back into the house.

He couldn't help but smile.

Kai padded into the kitchen wearing a violet housecoat. The patterned silk flowed behind him as he walked. Despite the thick belt tied into the neat bow holding it all together, the fabric fell loose over his rosy, tattooed shoulders.

Carried close to his chest like the little baby she was, Noon was curled up like a fluffy ball of snow. The cat purred happily and stared up at Kai with wide adoring eyes.

"What will we do with the bad man, hm?" Kai said. Eyeing Junsu, he pressed a kiss between Noon's happily twitching ears.

Junsu smiled at the scene they made but raised a brow at Kai's words.

"I'm the bad man?" he asked.

"Yes, Noon and I agreed on it," Kai replied, repositioning Noon in his arms to emphasize his point. The cat, no longer cradled in Kai's arms, was now staring at Junsu with her fluffy white legs dangling in the air, tail flicking happily this way and that.

Junsu had to resist snorting out a laugh. "I suppose some kind of punishment is in order then, hm?" At a languid pace, Junsu stepped up to Kai. He stood over the smaller man and when their eyes locked, he wet his lips. "What are you going to do with me? What do you have in mind?"

"Oh, I can think of plenty of things," Kai purred almost as loud as Noon.

"Kai, please," Junsu murmured even as a smirk curled one corner of his lips. He reached out, stroking Noon's ears back. "Not in front of the baby."

Noon blinked up at them, confused as ever.

With a soft laugh, Kai set the poor cat down The little snowball scurried off to continue watching her humans, safely hidden behind a boxy paper lamp.

Arms now free, Kai draped them over Junsu's shoulders as his Alpha approached.

Junsu's hands found Kai's trim waist. He slipped his fingers over the thick fabric of his robe's belt, teasing it loose ever so slowly.

"Jun."

Junsu met Kai's hooded gaze. "Yes?"

"It's first thing in the morning."

"If I remember correctly, you were the one who wanted to punish me. I just asked how you'd do it?"

With a long heavy sigh, Kai hugged Junsu closer and hung against his chest, putting all his weight on his Alpha's strong body.

"I'm too tired to punish you," he whined like a spoiled child. "It's too early."

Kai nuzzled against Junsu. He was worse than the cat, but it was kind of adorable.

"Raincheck?" Junsu laughed.

Kai hummed, resting his head against his Alpha's chest. He closed his eyes. Dark lashes brushed his cheeks. He was so beautiful.

Junsu couldn't help but move to kiss him. Kai responded in turn.

Their lips met, easy and sweet. Since they'd bonded, they both knew each other so well. They had barely left the bed after their arrival home. Junsu hadn't even given Kai the full tour yet.

Tired or not, a heady air was building between them. As the kiss deepened, they couldn't keep their hands off each other. Every caress felt right, every movement was perfect. When Kai slipped his tongue over Junsu's lips, it became clear they had to stop unless they wanted to end up back in bed for the rest of the day.

"You're right, it's too early," Junsu murmured, his voice a deep rumble reverberating from his chest. They'd been as ravenous as the newly bonded pair they were.

Junsu leaned back with great effort. "Do you want a cup of tea?" he asked.

When Junsu pulled away, Kai pouted. But then Junsu pressed another little peck to his lips and as soon as the chaste kiss broke, his expression cleared.

"Yes, please," Kai replied with a bright smile.

For a long time after that, neither of them could stop smiling.

Despite the stormy seas of their first meeting and the outside pressures that had forced them together, Junsu and Kai were happier than they'd ever been apart. It had been a long journey between empires and continents, a journey filled with misunderstandings, some intentional, some not. However, there wasn't a single thing they'd wish to cut out of the red thread of fate that had pulled them into each other's arms. Day and night, forever and always, every touch, every laugh, every smile would pull that unbreakable bond tighter.

About the Author

Sasha Hope is a lover of story, art, and design based in Canada. As a writer and an artist, she enjoys having the opportunity to create new characters and build new worlds for readers to explore. Having studied linguistics and a myriad of languages from a young age, she is passionate about including characters of different backgrounds in her work. Whether the setting is fantasy or reality, she believes that a diverse cast with diverse languages and cultures is a wonderful thing.

Crafting stories that embrace MM romance and erotica is her modus operandi. When she is not creating new worlds, she is travelling this one looking for inspiration or enjoying her career in the videogame industry.

Email
sasha.hope.writes@gmail.com

Facebook
www.facebook.com/sashahopewrites

Twitter
@SashaHopeWrites

Blog
www.the-empires-of-luxor-city.tumblr.com

Other NineStar books by this author

The Empires of Luxor City

Luxor City, a once lawless metropolis on the brink of civil war, is now at peace, but even in lighter times there are always shadows. In the technicolor streets of the Southern Empire, Junsu Sun, the Alpha heir to one of Luxor City's great crime families, busies himself by dealing with a blacklisted group known as the Underground.

After taking down one of the Underground's notorious leaders, Junsu assumes he'll be given time to rest and recuperate, but his mother, Alpha Xijuan Sun, has a new mission for him, involving a luxury cruise and a new mate, Omega Kaito Yamaguchi, of the powerful Yamaguchi family. Ever the dutiful son, Junsu obeys his orders as if it were any other mission, but this sort of engagement isn't exactly the type of thing he's used to and Kaito Yamaguchi certainly isn't the sort of Omega he's used to either.

Kaito is impatient, impassable, and impossible. He's a spoiled Omega who is pissed off that his family have reorganized his life and thrust him into this arranged mating with some Luxor City Alpha he's never met before. Kaito hasn't even seen a picture of Junsu Sun, a fact that Junsu uses to his advantage.

Faced with a week spent trapped on a luxury cruise with a rude, bratty Omega who doesn't even know who he is, Junsu decides to play a little trick on his future mate. But just how far will he let things go and where is the line between a little trick and a painful deception?

Meanwhile, other secrets floating between empires and continents are about to spill out onto the deck.

Also Available from NineStar Press

Connect with NineStar Press

www.ninestarpress.com

www.facebook.com/ninestarpress

www.facebook.com/groups/NineStarNiche

www.twitter.com/ninestarpress

www.ingramcontent.com/pod-product-compliance
Lightning Source LLC
Chambersburg PA
CBHW020629110726
47899CB00002B/707